The Latverian pebbles broke with satisfying ease.
Each flashed one last time as it shattered,
then fell dark.

Balsamo broke them into fragments, ground them into powder, and then ground them even more. When he was convinced that they no longer posed any hazard to him, he set his tools aside. The released energy added new scars to the pestle, but he didn't care about that.

His suite had a dining area and a small kitchen equipped with reasonable-quality china coffee mugs. He selected one, filled it with the coffee he'd bought downstairs, and added cream and sugar. Settling into an armchair, he sipped and considered the events of the day.

Casual conversations with the local bumpkins had included mentions of unexplainable events—screams, disappearances, lights in the sky. The newspaper files in the local library told of numerous mysterious deaths. He'd found five Latverian spirit stones in what was, by his standards, a mere knickknack shop.

Clearly, there was more to Sunnydale than met the eye.

Buffy the Vampire Slayer™

Available from SIMON & SCHUSTER

Afterimage

Pierce Askegren

**An original novel based on the hit television series
created by Joss Whedon**

SIMON SPOTLIGHT ENTERTAINMENT
New York London Toronto Sydney

This book is a work of fiction. Any references to historical events, real people, or real locales are used fictitiously. Other names, characters, places, and incidents are the product of the author's imagination, and any resemblance to actual events or locales or persons, living or dead, is entirely coincidental.

![SSE]

SIMON SPOTLIGHT ENTERTAINMENT

An imprint of Simon & Schuster Children's Publishing Division

1230 Avenue of the Americas, New York, New York 10020

™ & © 2006 Twentieth Century Fox Film Corporation. All rights reserved.

All rights reserved, including the right of reproduction in whole or in part in any form.

SIMON SPOTLIGHT ENTERTAINMENT and related logo are trademarks of Simon & Schuster, Inc.

Manufactured in the United States of America

First Edition 10 9 8 7 6 5 4 3 2 1

Library of Congress Control Number 2005933336

ISBN-13: 978-1-4169-1181-4

ISBN-10: 1-4169-1181-2

To Keith DeCandido

Special thanks to my editor, Patrick Price;
Emily Westlake; and my agent, Jennifer Jackson

Afterimage

Prologue

They'd thrown the place together in the 1950s, back when land and gas were cheap and no one had ever heard of a compact car. Scores of acres large, the Sunnydale Drive-In sat square in the center of a tract of land just outside the city limits, a reasonable distance from even the farthest houses. The relative isolation meant that the owners could go about their business without troubling the neighbors. Engine noises and fumes alike would be borne away on the night wind, and the light and glare of the movies' operation would inconvenience no one.

It had gone up fast and cheap, but in an era when things fast and cheap were still built to last. The main buildings had solid cinder-block walls reinforced with steel beams, and the plumbing and power lines were buried deep in armored conduits that still held up after decades of disuse. Even the huge screen, curved like a shield and facing the parking area, remained structurally sound. The screen's surface was a lost cause, of course, ruined by long years of exposure and no repair, but its supporting framework was perfectly serviceable.

The place's persistence was somewhat amazing, actually. There weren't many enterprises that could stand abandoned and unattended for so long and survive so well.

"They did good work," the contractor said. He was a big man, with beefy muscle that was slowly turning to fat and calloused hands that came with a career of physical labor. He parked his big pickup on the hill that overlooked the screen, got out, and unrolled the drive-in's original blueprints on his truck's hood. "Look," he said, indicating sections of the diagram. "Projection shack, concession stand, box office—they're all sound. Screen needs a new facing and the sound system will be updated, of course." He paused to glance at the bank loan officer who'd accompanied him in the ride out from Sunnydale. "You've got someone working the FCC thing, right?"

The loan officer nodded and dabbed sweat from his forehead. He wasn't in his element. It was a sunny afternoon and the fair skin of his bald scalp had already begun to redden. More perspiration darkened the shoulders and armpits of his suit. "The license should be ready by the time you finish installation," he said. The resurrected drive-in would use broadcast sound rather than car-side speakers, and the Federal

Communications Commission had to approve the equipment. "Assuming you can meet the deadline," he continued.

"Sure, no problem," responded the contractor. He spoke as if uttering a completely self-evident truth. "Run cables, patch pipes, landscape. Re-screen and install new signage. Marquee is a standard issue. Nothing big, really. My boys will have this place up and running in four weeks. Three if we run extra shifts."

"Four will be fine," the banker replied. He opened his briefcase atop the blueprint and began pulling out document folders. "Here," the banker said, handing them to the contractor one at a time. "You'll need these. Letter of credit, insurance forms, detailed specification sheets." Before handing over the last folder, he indicated the papers inside. "Contract. Sign and date."

It was quiet at the old drive-in. Even in the open vastness, the scratch of ballpoint pen was easily heard. As he signed his name, the contractor commented, "I hope you don't mind my saying this, but you don't seem very happy for a guy who's just been told that the job's a piece of cake."

"I'm sorry," the banker said. "I'm sure you'll do good work. I'm just not certain that reopening this place is a good idea. It has a history."

Chapter One

"**N**o," Buffy Summers said. She shook her head for emphasis, her blond hair rippling like water under the fluorescent lights. "I'm dead serious. He looked exactly like a penguin."

"Well, that doesn't sound very frightening," Willow Rosenberg replied. She looked skeptical. "I mean, penguins are friendly, formal fellows. They make children laugh! How much of a problem could a penguin be?"

They were at the big table in the Sunnydale High library. The school day had ended, but sometimes a slayer's day, like her work, was never done. Buffy, Willow, and Cordelia Chase were seated, but Giles stood, thumbing through one of his countless books and apparently not paying much attention to Buffy's report of the previous night's activities. Neither was Cordelia, who doodled idly on a composition book cover. But Willow was hanging on to

Buffy's every word about an encounter near the city zoo.

"Well, this *particular* penguin was eight feet tall, with fangs and claws," Buffy said. "Still formal—"

"—but not so friendly," Willow said, finishing her sentence.

Buffy nodded. Fangs and claws were nearly everyday factors in her life as the Slayer. But a giant-size penguin? Now that was something new. "Giles, ever hear about anything like that before? That's one for the books, right?"

For a man whose title was Watcher, Giles spent a lot of time listening. Without comment, he reversed the book he held, so that the three girls could see its opened pages.

One page was covered with tightly spaced lines of text in an ugly font. Opposite was an elaborate illustration of a gigantic penguin with fangs and claws. Beside it, evidently to indicate scale, was a human silhouette. The penguin-thing towered over the man.

"Oh," Buffy said meekly, as Giles resumed his reading.

"So, um, what did you do?" Willow asked. "You got him, right?"

Buffy nodded again. Pretty and well built, with large, expressive eyes that gleamed when she spoke, she often used gestures and motions to underscore her words.

"Well, the stake wouldn't do much good," Buffy said. "Those things have a thick layer of blubber or something—"

"Birds don't have blubber," Cordelia said smugly. They were her first words since joining the conclave, and it made sense that they'd be a correction.

Buffy and Willow blinked in unison. Cordelia wasn't particularly scholarly, and thus the tidbit of knowledge she offered so casually came as a bit of a surprise. Seeing their expressions, Cordelia explained. "Sixth grade book report." She tapped her temple with one elegant finger, clearly pleased to have pointed out Buffy's error. "Good memory. I'm not stupid, you know."

"Oh," Buffy said. Resolutely, she soldiered on. "He was coming at me pretty fast. When I had the chance, I reached inside his chest and kept reaching." She demonstrated with a pantomime, her arm extended and open fingers wiggling.

Willow's eyes bulged. Buffy made a note to herself to cut back on the graphic detail. As with the fangs and claws thing, she'd become so accustomed to the nuts and bolts of her work that she sometimes forgot how squeamish civilians could be. And although Willow wasn't quite a civilian, she wasn't a slayer, either. As for Cordelia . . .

To be perfectly honest, Buffy wasn't entirely sure what role Cordelia Chase had in her life these days. They'd disliked each other since Buffy's first day at Sunnydale High, but recent events had cast the Slayer and the shallow beauty queen as reluctant allies.

But she could worry about that later, Buffy decided.

"I kept reaching," she continued, limiting her

account to words, not reenactment, "until I found something hard, and then I squeezed it. The thing made a burp—"

"Real penguins make a sound like a crow's caw," Cordelia said.

"—and then he kind of melted," Buffy said. She favored Cordelia with a sharp look. "I don't suppose regular penguins do that, either?"

"What became of the remains?" Giles asked.

Buffy shrugged. "There are storm drains all over that courtyard," she said. "Last I saw, Frosty was dripping into one. It rained this morning, too. I don't think anything was left behind."

Giles nodded, closing his book. Buffy wasn't sure whether he was relieved because of strategic concerns or simply because he was a tidy man.

"Wait until Xander hears about this," Willow said excitedly.

"Where is Xander, anyway?" Cordelia asked. She set down her pen. "That boy's been making himself pretty scarce lately after school."

Willow looked mildly confused. "When did you start keeping tabs on Xander?"

Before Cordelia could respond the library doors opened and the subject of Willow's question sauntered in. Xander Harris was tall and dark-haired, and usually looked mildly bemused by the world around him. He had good features and better eyes. He grinned as he entered, book bag under one arm and a thick sheaf of papers under the other.

"Hey there, groovy guys and groovy gals," he said,

dropping into an empty chair on Cordelia's side of the table. He continued, "Oh, and Giles, too."

"Speak of the devil," Cordelia said.

"You know, Cordy, that's the kind of thing you probably shouldn't say," Xander said. "I mean, since we live on top of the Hellmouth and all." He dropped his book bag to the floor and placed his sheaf of papers facedown on the table in front of him. It was a two-inch stack of orange sheets, clamped together with a heavy binder clip.

"Where have *you* been?" Buffy asked.

Xander made a wry expression. "Had to pick up an extra-credit assignment," he said. "I really blew that history quiz Monday."

"Not just now," Buffy said. "You've been making yourself scarce lately." Not only had Xander nearly missed the current gathering of friends and associates—the Scoobies—he'd completely missed several promised study sessions during the preceding two weeks. And if Xander didn't study, he didn't do well on quizzes. It was one of the secret laws of the universe.

"After-school job," Xander said. He seemed inordinately pleased with himself. "Two or three hours a day and I have enough for comic books, video games, and big bowls of Skittles."

Xander could talk for a long time about junk food and other ephemera. Before he could go any further down that conversational path, Buffy asked, "Where are you working, Xander?"

Xander proudly unclipped the stack of papers he'd

brought and passed the orange sheets around. His voice took on the cadence of a carnival barker as he said, "Check it out, check it out, something you will enjoy."

It was a handbill. Halftone images made up the background, clearly of actors and actresses in character, a few of whom Buffy recognized. Overlaid on the collage were increasingly larger lines of type, announcing:

Grand Opening! Grand Opening!!
Grand Opening!!!
The Return of a Great Tradition!
Go to the Drive-In and Have Yourselves a Treat!
Dusk to Dawn Thrillerama Festival of Fun!
Free Corn Dogs and Cola for Late-Stayers!

Next came a list of movies. Giles and the girls read the titles, then stared at Xander with expressions that ranged from confusion to disdain, with many stops in between.

"Great, huh?" Xander asked, obviously delighted and expecting them to be too. "*Double Drunken Dragon Kung Fu Fight* is the one for me!"

"*Mysteries of Chainsaw Mansion*?" Buffy asked skeptically.

"It's a horror movie," Xander said helpfully.

"Not for me, thanks," Buffy said. "I've got enough problems."

"What is this?" Cordelia asked. "*The Lonely Cheerleader*? That's ridiculous! Cheerleaders are *never* lonely!"

"You should know," Xander said, slightly crest-fallen. He reached to reclaim the handbill, but she pulled it away.

"Oh, I don't know," Willow said. She pushed back a stray lock of coppery hair. "Some of these look pretty interesting. What's *Caged Blondes* about?"

"It's a women-in-prison movie," Xander said. Much of his habitual good cheer had ebbed, but not all of it. "Good woman, accused of a crime she didn't commit, has to fight her way to freedom. They used to be a staple of drive-ins."

"Which brings us, inexorably, to the next question," Giles said. He sounded patient. He was very good at making patience sound like exasperation, though. "What on earth is a drive-in?"

"Hey, yeah, that's right, G. You're from Jolly Old England," Xander said, as if he'd just remembered.

"Yes, Xander, I am," Giles said, sounding even more patient, which meant that he wasn't.

"I guess they don't have drive-ins there," Xander said. Primarily for the Watcher's benefit, he offered up a quick history of drive-ins and drive-in movies. The theaters sprung up early in the twentieth century, as a relatively low-tech, low-investment means of exhibition. They hit their stride in the 1950s, with the emergence of teenagers as a specific marketing niche. Their popularity started to fade out late in the 1970s, and though some drive-ins lingered, they were few and far between.

"Home video and rising gas prices conspired to make the business impractical," Xander concluded.

"You've been reading again," Buffy said. She pursed her lips in a mock kiss. "I'm so proud of you!"

Xander looked at her blankly.

"I can tell when you're quoting a reference work," she said. "Your face screws up and I can hear the gears spin in your head." She made a mechanical sound.

"Reading is all well and good," Giles said, handing the sheet back as if he were concerned it might bite him, "but what does this have to do with any of us?"

"The old Sunnydale Drive-In is reopening," Xander said. He took the sheet and returned it to his stack, then reluctantly accepted Buffy's and Cordelia's. Willow kept hers. "I've been working at the construction site," he said, then corrected himself. "The re-construction site, I guess. You know, doing coffee and meal runs, sweeping up, that sort of thing." He indicated his stack of handbills. "I'm supposed to distribute these."

"So you're a flunky," Cordelia said tartly. Sometimes it seemed to Buffy that Cordelia said *everything* tartly.

"I prefer to think of myself as a 'diversified assistant,'" Xander responded.

"A gopher," Buffy said. "You *gophe* for things."

"If you must put it like that," Xander said.

"I think it's a nice way to put it," Willow said. "Gophers are adorable."

Remarkably, Xander blushed. There were times when Willow could make him do that, if she said just the right thing at the right moment. "Anyway, Boss-man says he's had success in other cities, with festivals and retrospectives. Pick up the facilities for a song, slap some new paint on the place, and voilà!"

He beamed. No one beamed back at him. If none of the other four looked confused anymore, none of them looked particularly interested, either, with the possible exception of Willow. Oblivious, Xander rambled on. "Even better," he said, "I've got passes. Grand opening is this Friday, and you're all invited. On me!"

"This is at night, right?" Buffy asked.

"Yeah, of course," Xander said. He looked wounded by the question, or mildly offended, or some mixture of the two. "Can't watch movies outside in broad daylight."

"I have a date," she said.

"Oh?" Cordelia asked coolly.

"Angel?" Xander asked.

"Mr. Pointy," Buffy said. She cocked her head and leaned in Xander's direction. "Hello?" she asked. "Patrol, remember? 'Dusk to dawn' kind of gets in the way, even if it looks like something I'd enjoy." She paused. "Which I don't think it does, really. *Caged Blondes*?"

"Oh. Right."

"Sorry," Buffy said, managing to sound regretful— not filled with sorrow, but sorry to have disappointed him.

"How about you, Cordelia?" Xander asked.

"I'll be busy too," she said.

"Date?" he asked, sounding a little bit worried.

"Now, Xander, where do I usually go on Fridays? Hmmmm?" Cordelia asked. When he continued to look at her blankly, she explained. "The Bronze. It's girls' night out."

"Well, maybe Harmony and Aura—"

"Oh, yeah," Cordelia said with mild sarcasm, interrupting as he named her friends. "They'd be up for a night out with you. And movies like *these*. Uh-huh. Sure."

Willow raised her hand with just a bit of timidity. She wiggled her fingers for attention, but no one seemed to notice. Xander and Cordelia, especially, were too busy trading half glares.

Giles cleared his throat. When no one noticed that, either, he cleared it again, loudly. "Ahem," he said, secure in his audience at last. "As fascinating as all of this is, I think it's time to turn our attention to more substantive matters than American entertainments. When you made your belated entrance, Xander, Buffy was regaling us with her exploits on patrol last night. Perhaps she'd like to resume?"

Buffy liked. "There's not much more, really," she said. "After the penguin melted . . ."

He looked like a slender Santa Claus as he window-shopped his way along Sunnydale's Main Street. The man had white hair, thick and wavy, and a matching white beard that was bushy and big, but still neatly styled. He had an air of self-importance, but without any hostility or arrogance; he nodded politely at passersby and consistently yielded the right of way to women and children. He wore a nicely tailored suit and an open-necked dress shirt that looked like silk, and

Amanda Hoch was certain that his Italian loafers cost more than she could earn in a year.

Amanda was in full regalia herself. She was wearing her favorite black outfit and silver accessories, with a fresh purple rinse in her hair and her skin painstakingly paled with cosmetics. She stood in the entranceway alcove of the Magic Box, where she worked, sucking down the last of a clove cigarette. It was only Amanda's fifth week in Sunnydale (her second week on the job), and she was still getting the lay of the land. She watched approaching strangers the same way she did most things in this town: with wary suspicion.

Even seen from a distance, the man appeared entirely too genial and pleasant. She didn't like people who smiled easily, or who seemed so at home in the bright sunlight. She had a cultivated fondness for dark things and shadows, which was why she'd applied for the part-time job at the Magic Box. So far, however, the gig was a disappointment, like so much of her life. She spent most of her eight poorly compensated hours a day selling tacky items to New Age wannabes and Wiccan poseurs, who were surprisingly plentiful in the local population. At least the white-haired guy didn't look like he was another one of *those*.

He *was* headed for the Magic Box, though. Just in time, Amanda dropped the cigarette butt and ground it beneath one booted foot. She opened the door and stepped aside so that the potential customer could enter.

"Thank you, miss," the stranger said, taking the door and waving her in. His voice was warm and gentle, in an accent as Italian as his loafers. "I'd like to look around a bit."

"Make yourself at home," Amanda said as she returned to her station at the cash register. In seconds she was engrossed in her magazine again, though not so engrossed that she didn't glance occasionally in the man's direction. The Magic Box had some pricey wares, after all. Little things that fit easily into pockets. The well-heeled bearded man didn't look like a shoplifter, but you could never tell.

The place was new to him. Amanda could tell that, even with her brief tenure. The stranger browsed the Magic Box's merchandise like an explorer, giving each shelf and display a cursory glance before moving on to the next. He touched little but leaned close to read book spines and jar labels. He was working his way along the bins of herbs when he finally broke the silence.

"A surprisingly well-stocked establishment," he said. "It seems out of place in a town like this."

"Sunnydale is full of surprises," Amanda said sourly, still trying to read. Despite herself, she continued, "You would not *believe* some of the things I've heard about since I got here. I sure don't."

"Ah," the man said, "you're a newcomer?"

Amanda nodded. Despite her initial distaste for his general manner, she found herself warming to him. "A little more than a month," she said. "My grandmother needed some live-in help with my grandfather."

"I thought so," the man said, smiling again. "I didn't think you were from around here."

"The look, you mean?" Amanda asked. She waggled black-nailed fingers and flashed a smile, black-lipped and brief.

There were other Goths in Sunnydale, but not so many that Amanda didn't cause comment. That was one reason she refused to give up the look, despite her grandmother's pleas. Her appearance was a statement, a demonstration of individuality and rebellion. Amanda liked standing out in a white-bread world.

"It was the dialect, actually," the man said. He stood next to the shop's main cabinet now, where high-ticket items hid behind locked glass. "New Jersey," he continued. "Paramus, I think."

Amanda was impressed. "Wow. How did you know that?"

"Dialect. Regional variations in a language, specifically word choices and pronunciations," the man said. He gestured at the locked case. "I wonder if I might see the crystals?"

Usually Amanda disliked fooling with the display case. Not this time, though—not for this customer. She dug out the keys, knelt, and worked the lock. "I thought I had an accent," Amanda said.

The crystals he'd indicated were square cut and five in number. They rested on a black velvet presentation board. Amanda took the board from the case and set it on the display case's top so that he could inspect them.

He looked, but didn't touch. They glinted slightly as he eyed them. "No," he said. "Accents are when two languages impact on one another. You speak with a distinctive dialect, my dear; *I* have an accent."

It was precisely the sort of mini-lecture that Amanda had always found irritating in the extreme, but somehow the white-haired man made the information sound interesting, even useful. Wanting to repay the favor, she read from the card that accompanied the crystals.

"Latverian Spirit Stones," she read aloud. "Premiere quality, certified. They respond to human psycho-etheric potentials." She'd never had to show the gems closely before, and she stumbled over some of the words. The instructions on how to use the things were clear enough, though.

Amanda took one stone in her hand. It was as slick as water against her skin. In the crystal's depths, the slight glint of a moment before became something brighter, a spark that danced and shone brightly. The stone's surface remained perfectly cool.

"Wow," Amanda said. She'd never thought any of the stuff in the Magic Box would actually work. She looked up. "Wanna try it?" she asked.

The man smiled and drew back slightly from the offered stones. "I don't think so," he said. "I'm satisfied that they're genuine. I'll take the set."

"All of them?" Amanda asked as she set down the stone. She blinked. The crystals were very expensive, among the dearest items in the shop.

"All five," the man agreed. He smiled and his pale blue eyes twinkled, reminding her of the crystal's surprising gleam. "Unless there are more?"

There weren't. Amanda packaged the five stones

carefully. Each went into its own locked case, then the five cases went into a larger box, to be secured with packing tape and then deposited neatly into a handled bag bearing the store logo. She rang up the sale and accepted a credit card the color of platinum. Amanda dawdled slightly at each step, far from eager to conclude the transaction.

"Here you go," she said with her very best smile as she passed the charge slip to him for his signature. "Will you be in Sunnydale long, Mr. Belasimo?"

"Balsamo," he corrected her, but so gently that it didn't sound like a correction at all. "Bal-sa-mo. And no, my dear, not for very long. Once my business concludes, I shall depart."

"Oh," Amanda said, trying to hide her disappointment. "Well, I hope to see you again."

"Perhaps you shall," Balsamo said. Then, unexpectedly, he took her right hand and kissed her fingers.

It was a flourish that Amanda had seen before in movies but never in real life. She had no idea of any proper way to respond, so all she could do was smile silently and blush a bit as he turned and exited with his purchase.

More than an hour passed before she could fully return her attention to the magazine. Something about the transaction affected her, and the effect lingered. It wasn't the man's easy knowledge, or his elegance and grace, or even the fact that he'd spent more in ten minutes than the Magic Box took in during most weeks. It was something else, something subtler.

He'd treated her like a lady, Amanda finally realized. He'd made her feel like she was someone special, and not just a Goth shopgirl from New Jersey.

Balsamo forgot about the guttersnipe behind the counter before taking ten steps outside. No, not forgot; rather, he took and filed her image safely away from his consciousness. His knowledge of the purple-haired girl's existence remained available, should he ever need to call upon it, but the distaste he felt no longer distracted him. He had taught himself the mental trick in his youth, and it had proved essential over the many years that followed.

The peasants he shared the walkway with received much the same attention. He nodded politely at other men, stepped aside for the ladies, and made himself smile at the children, and then drove them all from his thoughts. They didn't matter. All that mattered was the paper sack he gripped in his left hand.

He'd been very fortunate, he realized. He never would have imagined that a place like Sunnydale would hold a genuine spirit stone, let alone five of them. Balsamo would have liked to know how the five glistening bits of crystal had made their way to the New World, and to this insipid little township. Perhaps later, after his primary business was done, he'd return to the Magic Box to research the matter.

He imagined that he could make the purple-haired wench tell him anything he wanted to know. Likely, he'd enjoy the process too.

Balsamo's stride was long and brisk. It took him only minutes to traverse the six blocks between the shop and his hotel. He smiled at the doorman as he entered, smiled again at the concierge, and then checked at the front desk for messages. There were none, so he proceeded to his room, pausing only to purchase a Styrofoam container of coffee from the lobby shop. He disliked the local blend but disliked brewing his own even more.

A small suitcase waited for him in his penthouse suite. He inspected its seals carefully before opening it. It was the only piece of luggage that had not been unpacked, and it pleased him to see that none of the hotel staff had been foolish enough to tamper with it. The case was small, but its interior was efficiently designed and held a score of interesting instruments. After considering his options for a moment, he decided that the simplest method would be best.

It usually was, of course.

He chose a small mortar and pestle, each hewn from ivory that was once a dragon's tooth. Both implements were marked with mystic symbols and discolored from heavy use. They'd been in Balsamo's possession for a very long time.

He unwrapped the purchased stones. One by one they lit up like small suns when he touched them for the first time. They flared brightly enough to singe the skin of his fingertips and make his eyes water, but Balsamo scarcely noticed. He dropped them into the dragon-tooth mortar, applying the pestle as he muttered ancient words of power, and then went to work.

The Latverian pebbles broke with satisfying ease. Each flashed one last time as it shattered, then fell dark. Balsamo broke them into fragments, ground them into powder, and then ground them even more. When he was convinced that they no longer posed any hazard to him, he set his tools aside. The released energy added new scars to the pestle, but he didn't care about that.

His suite had a dining area and a small kitchen equipped with reasonable-quality china coffee mugs. He selected one, filled it with the coffee he'd bought downstairs, and added cream and sugar. Settling into an armchair, he sipped and considered the events of the day.

Casual conversations with the local bumpkins had included mentions of unexplainable events—screams, disappearances, lights in the sky. The newspaper files in the local library told of numerous mysterious deaths. He'd found five Latverian spirit stones in what was, by his standards, a mere knickknack shop.

Clearly, there was more to Sunnydale than met the eye.

Chapter Two

Dinner at the Summers house that night was comfort food, as it often was. Joyce Summers's marriage had ended badly, and although many aspects of traditional family life had fallen by the wayside in the years since, Joyce refused to let go of them all. After coming to Sunnydale in search of a fresh start, she always tried to make the evening meal a sort of capstone for the day. She wanted it to be a time when she and Buffy could sit and talk and, hopefully, reinforce their bonds. That meant sitting together at the big dining room table, eating solid and substantial food, using real plates and real utensils. Paper cartons, Styrofoam cups, and plastic sporks seldom visited the Summers residence, if Joyce had anything to say about it.

Unless she was very, very busy.

She allowed the first minute or two of the meal to pass in near-silence. She liked watching Buffy eat.

There was something reassuringly basic about it. And Buffy could eat an astonishing amount. Joyce knew that teenagers had healthy appetites, but her daughter seemed to have a bottomless hunger. Given that the younger Summers didn't seem to have much interest in sports, it was a wonder that the girl was able to keep herself so trim.

Finally, Joyce allowed herself to ask the question. "So," she said, "how was school today, dear?"

"Gloomph!" Buffy said. She chewed rapidly and swallowed. "Good," she repeated, before shoveling more chicken casserole into her mouth.

"Did you learn anything?" Joyce asked.

Buffy shrugged. Joyce supposed that a shrug was about as much of an answer as she would have given her own mother, back in the day.

"Did anything interesting happen?" Joyce asked. She tried not to sound needy.

Buffy took a crusty roll and broke it, then spread butter on the fleecy whiteness inside. As she worked, she spoke. "Kind of," she said. "Someone detonated a frog in bio. Willow thinks she's figured out a new file transfer protocol, but I can't tell what she's talking about. Xander got a job."

"Detonated a frog?" Joyce asked. She set her forkful of food down for a moment.

Buffy shrugged again. "Dunno," she said. "Wasn't my lab section it happened in."

"Oh." For some reason Joyce felt relieved. She wouldn't want her little girl to see something so gruesome. "Oh, well, that's better. What about Xander?"

"What about him?" Buffy asked. She ate half her buttered roll with a single, engulfing bite and set the remainder on her plate.

"You said he'd gotten a job," Joyce said. Xander was one of Buffy's friends, but beyond that, she wasn't sure what role the Harris boy played in her daughter's life. From what little she'd seen of them together, there didn't seem to be any kind of romance in progress, though she had a hunch Xander wished differently. "What kind of job?"

"He's a flunky. No, a gopher. We agreed he's a gopher," Buffy said. "That's not as good as a flunky but better than a minion." She was still focused almost entirely on her meal. Asparagus spears disappeared into her mouth with amazing rapidity.

"Don't bolt your food, dear," Joyce said patiently. She generally looked forward to each evening meal with her daughter, but sometimes she wondered why.

"They're reopening the Sunnydale Drive-In," Buffy said by way of explanation.

"Oh. That's right," Joyce said. "I heard about that. I wonder if that's such a good idea."

Now she had Buffy's attention. The blond teenager paused and looked at her mom. "Oh, yeah?" she said.

Joyce nodded. "They were talking about it at the gallery today," she said. "One of our bank's loan officers has the property's account. He's working with the people reopening the place." She sipped her iced tea. "Barney's lived here a long time. He says that place has a history of trouble."

"Barney?" Buffy asked. She snickered, with the

easy cruelty of youth. "You actually know someone named *Barney*? Is he a caveman or a purple dinosaur?"

"Barney is very nice," Joyce said, in mild reproof. More than once in recent years it had occurred to Joyce that the day might come when the name Buffy would be considered quaint or goofy. "He has the gallery's account too. I like him."

A worried expression flickered across Buffy's features. No, not worried, wary. The look of mild apprehension came and went so fast that a casual observer might have missed it. Not Joyce, however. Joyce had seen that look before. Buffy could be remarkably mature about some things, but she tended to view her mother's occasional forays into the dating scene with some trepidation.

That was understandable, considering how some of those forays had played out.

"Not like that," Joyce said, half-honestly.

"Oh," Buffy said. "Okay." She helped herself to more casserole and set about making it disappear. "Tell me about the drive-in," she said between mouthfuls.

"Barney says they shut it down about twenty years ago," Joyce said. She ate some of her own meal. The asparagus spears were fresh and tender, bought at a farmers' market and poached in chicken broth. They tasted good. "Home video and the rise in gas prices—"

"—conspired to make the business impractical," Buffy interrupted.

Joyce looked at her, one eyebrow raised in silent interrogation.

"Xander," Buffy explained.

Joyce sighed. She wasn't surprised. Xander was a veritable wellspring of pop-culture trivia. Sometimes she wondered how anyone could know so much useless information.

"They're not gone completely," Joyce said. "And sometimes they come back."

"Sounds pretty retro to me," Buffy said. "And not in a good way. What's the appeal?"

Joyce thought back to her teenage years. She thought about one of her earliest dates, with a boy whose name she'd long forgotten. They'd sat in the front seat of her parents' car, eating bad concession-stand food and watching bad movies. The night air had been clean and cool, and the world had still seemed bright and exciting.

"It was fun," was all that Joyce could think to say. It seemed very distant.

"Sounds like someone paid a visit to Lovers' Lane," Buffy said, slightly mocking. Her wariness about Joyce's social life didn't preclude some teasing.

"It wasn't like that," Joyce said sharply. It was, actually, but she wasn't about to provide her daughter with the details.

"What about the bugs?" Buffy asked. An odd pragmatism was part of her character.

"Bugs?"

"Bugs," Buffy said, nodding. "Pesky things. They drink blood. Lovers' Lane plus bright movie screen must have been mosquito heaven. Didn't you get eaten alive?"

Joyce hadn't thought about the bugs. Rather than

answer, she sipped her iced tea again. It was from a powder, but the fresh lemon she'd added made it better.

Evidently realizing that she wasn't going to get the answer she wanted, Buffy asked another question. "What about the trouble, then?"

"Trouble?"

Buffy quoted her mother's own words back to her. "'Barney says that place has a history of trouble.'"

Joyce shrugged. "I don't know what he meant, Buffy," she said, a bit sadly. "He didn't say and I didn't ask. I'd heard the same kind of thing so many times before. It seems that every street and every institution in this town has a history of trouble." She paused. "I like Sunnydale, honey, but sometimes I wonder."

"You're not going to move us again, are you?" Buffy asked. She looked anxious. "Don't even think about it!"

"No, of course not," Joyce said reassuringly. "You're happy here, aren't you?"

"I'm fine, Mom," Buffy said. She took a third helping of the entrée. Joyce wondered again where the girl put it all. "My grades are okay, and I haven't fallen in with the wrong set." She grinned, and the expression lit up her face. Her words sounded only slightly forced as she continued. "These days I even hang with Cordelia Chase, the most popular gal in town. I'm with the in crowd, baby!"

"I suppose," Joyce said. Like most mothers, she had done a little research on her daughter's friends, both by meeting them and by asking around. Xander, for example, seemed nice enough, a bit clownish; from what she'd heard of his parents, he could use a good friend, and he had one in Buffy. Joyce wasn't sure that anyone could consider Buffy's immediate circle the "in crowd," but they all seemed to be good kids.

The meal stretched on in relative silence after that, interrupted only by sporadic exchanges about the food, and similar niceties. It was only over dessert (gelatin for Joyce, chocolate cake for Buffy) that the subject of school arose again.

"I need to go out for a bit," Buffy said. The announcement was no surprise. Buffy went out most nights.

"I'd hoped you would stay in tonight, dear," Joyce said. "I hardly ever see you anymore."

Buffy pressed on. "Willow wants some help with the computer thingy," she said. "And then I thought we might go to the Bronze afterward."

"It's a school night," Joyce said. The protest was mild and probably futile, but it had become nearly ritual. Joyce wasn't sure she liked the Bronze, or approved of the sheer amount of time Buffy spent there.

"Aw, c'mon, Mom," Buffy said, in a lightly mocking tone. She started to clear the table. "All the *cool* kids will be there!"

Joyce sighed. She felt fresh sympathy for her own mother, and what she must have gone through, long years before. Who could really know what kind of lives their children led?

The night was alive. Something was going to happen, Buffy knew, even if she wasn't precisely sure how she knew. The half-moon hung low in a cloudless sky, and the air was clear and cool for an early autumn night.

Buffy sometimes joked to her friends about her "Slayer-sense." It was the kind of pop-culture allusion that prompted Xander to nod knowingly and Giles to roll his eyes in mild disgust, but sometimes the joke wasn't a joke at all. Sometimes she actually seemed to feel a charge in the air, an electric crackle that made her scalp itch like a bad perm, promising imminent menace. She felt it now as she paced the familiar course of her patrol. When the occasional passerby approached, she took pains to conceal her miniature crossbow in the oversize handbag that did double duty as a weapons cache, but her favorite stake never left her hand.

Her rounds included many of Sunnydale's known psychic hot spots: the empty warehouse that often sheltered a nest of vampires, the deconsecrated church that was headquarters for a coven of devil worshippers, and the seedy strip of taverns rumored to cater to the paranormal crowd. The list went on and on, and Buffy inspected each locus without incident.

She was in the cemetery when something finally happened. Between crypt and neighboring tree, something moved toward her with smooth, liquid grace. She saw it from the corner of one eye and instinctively spun, raising her crossbow.

"Oh," Buffy said. "It's you."

"Hey," Angel said. His voice was soft, and he lifted his hands in mock-surrender. He was dressed in his habitual black, slacks and shirt and leather jacket, and his handsome features were fair under the half-moon's pale light.

"Hey, yourself," Buffy said, looking at him, still wary. She felt as if little elves with sandpaper shoes were dancing on her nerves. Something was still wrong.

"What's up, Buffy?" the vampire asked. He sounded concerned. His hands remained raised.

"Not lots," Buffy said. "Helped Willow with some homework, or tried to. Told Mom I was going to the Bronze, but I decided that this would be *lots* more fun than hanging with my peers and scoping out the music scene." She gave him a wry half smile. Being the Slayer meant lying to her mother fairly often, and she didn't entirely enjoy that part of the job.

"Um," Angel said hesitantly. "Okay."

"How about you?" she asked lightly. "What's up?"

"Well, your crossbow is, for one thing," Angel said. The weapon's bolt was trained precisely at his stilled heart.

"Oh!" Buffy said, chagrined. She lowered the weapon with hasty embarrassment. "Reflex action and all that," she continued. "You know, patrol, tombstones, mysterious stranger—"

Immediately she wished she could take back the words. Whatever Angel was, he was no stranger. They'd been through too much together for her to ever call him that.

He *was* mysterious, though. There were endless mysteries in his eyes.

"Yeah," Angel said. "But reflex usually doesn't go on this long. Look at you. You're still on edge."

He was right. Though she'd lowered the crossbow to her side, her trigger finger remained curled around the weapon's release, as if of its own accord. Buffy's muscles were prepared for instant action. It was classic fight-or-flight stuff, not the kind of response she typically felt in Angel's presence.

"Something's in the air," she said. "Something's going to happen, I think. Don't know what."

"You think?" Angel smiled. He was hundreds of years old, she knew, but the expression made his eternally youthful features seem positively boyish.

"Yeah."

"Buffy, you're the Slayer. You live on top of the Hellmouth. Something's *always* happening," Angel said.

"Good point," she said. She forced herself to relax, at least incrementally. She even smiled. "Walk with me for a while, then."

Somewhere in the distance a dog howled. At least, Buffy thought it was a dog. She *hoped* it was just a dog. Buffy's nights on patrol were exercises in contradiction. Night after night she went out looking for trouble, hoping she wouldn't find it.

There were times, though, when life seemed normal. This was one, and she didn't want it to change. Walking through a cool autumn night with a good looking guy, her footfalls matching rhythm with his, talking about their days and lives—what could be more normal than that?

She was a child of ancient prophecy, likely to live a short life with a brutal end. The most interesting guy in her life was a creature of the night, a vampire with a heart that could love but did not beat, prisoner of a curse.

Oh yeah, there was that. But did any of it really matter?

Right now, alone with Angel in the moonlight, Buffy didn't think so. Her eyes continued to search the shadows, but bit by bit the worst of the tension oozed away as she told Angel about her day. He made her feel secure and safe simply with his presence.

"Detonated a frog?" he asked. She knew that he'd seen much worse—they both had—but he was polite enough to make an expression of amused distaste. "Well, boys will be boys."

Buffy nodded. "Except I don't think it was a boy who did it," she said.

"What else happened?" he asked as they approached one of the cemetery's aboveground crypts. Some family had failed to keep pace with the grounds-keeping fees, and the tomb had fallen into a state of mild disrepair. The brass hardware was weathered and dull, and clinging ivy half-covered one wall.

"Else?" Buffy asked. "Must there always be an else?"

"There's always something else," he said lightly.

"Oh, Xander got a job," she said brightly. "He's a gopher at the drive-in."

"The drive-in?" Angel asked.

The last thing she wanted to do right now was talk

to him about another guy. She wondered if he felt the same. This close, she could tell that he wasn't breathing. Vampires didn't have to, except for speech.

And it didn't matter that his heart wasn't beating, either. Hers was working hard enough for both of them.

"It's a long story," Buffy said. She paused midstep and turned to look at him. There was an old oak next to the tomb, and the moonlight shining down through the tree's branches did interesting things to Angel's face. She leaned closer and gazed into his eyes.

"Feeling better now?" Angel asked.

Buffy nodded. "Much, " she said. She made a dismissive gesture. "Meemies all gone."

"Maybe you just need to switch to decaf," he said.

"Maybe," she said. "Or perhaps I need something else."

Angel's skin felt cool when she placed her hands on his cheeks, but it warmed quickly. She pulled his face closer to hers, her lips parting. It was a perfect moment, and she didn't want anything to spoil it.

Then, with a snarl, something rudely did.

Inside the Bronze the night was alive. The air was scented with fog and sweat, and throbbed with the beat of the band. The ensemble *du noir* was a plucky band of traditionalists, performing under the cryptic acronym TDQYDJP. A helpful placard explained that the abbreviation stood for "The Don't Quit Your Day Job Players." The group played mostly cover tunes— plain vanilla rock, but they played loud enough and well enough to satisfy the scores of teens crowded onto the club's worn dance floor. Kids were dancing and bouncing and gyrating with force sufficient enough to send tremors through the place's infrastructure, but Cordelia was not one of them. She wasn't in the Bronze tonight to dance, but to hold court.

She had secured a good table on the main level, situated to provide a good vantage point but far enough away from the stage that she could hear herself speak. She'd permitted the other members of her personal troika, Harmony and Aura, to join her. They sat on either side of her like mismatched bookends, hanging on her every word. Together the three passed judgment on the band, their drinks, the other Bronze patrons, and anything else that piqued their interest.

Sitting in judgment had long been one of Cordelia's preferred pastimes. Someone had to do it, after all, and she couldn't imagine anyone better qualified. She had the upbringing and refinement to assess the poor boobs that swarmed through her life, and it would have been a shame not to share her insights. Harmony and Aura had similarly good taste (though not as highly developed, of course), and they made good companions on her judicial bench. For years the three of them had moved through life together, in study halls and in classrooms, in restaurants and on the playing field, telling the world the way it was supposed to be. In recent months, since her growing involvement with Buffy and the others, the pastime's charm had started fading, but it was far from gone.

"Look, Cordy," Harmony said. She was a pretty

blonde, much blonder than Buffy, and she tended to echo Cordelia's every observation. It was seldom that she made one of her own. "Look at the guy with three chins. Purple-hair there is going to shoot him down!"

Cordy followed Harmony's gaze. The Bronze didn't allow stage-diving, but the more hardcore members of the audience still tended to congregate near the stage's lip. There, only a few feet from the TDQYDJP's booming woofer, a portly gent who had unwisely shaved his head was saying something to a Goth chick with purple hair.

Cordelia didn't much like Goth chicks. She could see the value of making a statement, but surely there were better ones to make. And that amount of makeup had to be murder on the skin. Plus, her outings with Buffy and the Scoobies had made her wary of dark-clad creatures with the wrong color hair.

"How long do you give him?" Aura asked. She had dark bronze skin and black hair, and she generally showed a bit more initiative than Harmony. She was at least as blasé, however. Even before Cordelia, Aura had stumbled briefly into the occult war that had chosen Sunnydale as its battlefield, when she discovered the body of one of that war's victims.

"Seven seconds," Cordelia said, without pausing to consider. She'd been playing this game for a long time.

". . . six, five, four, three, two . . . ," Harmony and Aura chanted in perfect unison.

Precisely on "zero" the purple-haired girl's hand came up in a short, fast arc. When her hand stopped, the drink she held splashed in the bald guy's face. A security goon, drawn by the disturbance, approached to escort them both away from the stage.

"There's trouble in paradise," Cordelia said, as Harmony and Aura laughed. They sounded like magpies in stereo.

The three of them carried on like that for an hour or so, but Cordelia was bored by the twenty-minute mark. She turned down three invitations to dance and accepted one, but when the guy wanted to do more than that, she ditched him and returned to the table. During the break between sets, the band's percussionist approached and invited all of them backstage. Harmony and Aura agreed eagerly, only to backtrack when they heard Cordelia decline. The band was a good act and they made good music, but Mrs. Chase's little girl wasn't going anywhere with rockers who hadn't at *least* made the Billboard Top 100.

"Hel-lo," Aura said, as Cordelia bade the TDQYDJP emissary good-bye. "There's a fresh face in town."

Threading his way through the milling crowd on the dance floor was someone Cordelia had never seen before. Tall and Mediterranean dark, he was handsome in an insolently casual way, with heavy-lidded dark eyes and black hair styled in an elaborate pompadour. He wore old-style biker's leathers, festooned with buckles and straps, and he moved with the grace of a jungle cat.

As Cordelia watched, it hit her that the stranger was hot. No, he was *Hot,* and he knew it.

"Yum," Aura said softly.

"Yum, indeed," Cordelia agreed. There was no

denying it. Oddly, though, she found herself only slightly intrigued by the newcomer. One reason was what she coined "the Xander situation"; the other was something else.

Cordelia recalled when another leather-clad stranger, tall and dark and handsome, had drifted into the Bronze late one rockin' night. She had all but thrown herself at him, only to draw back in chagrin when he'd brushed her aside. That stranger proved to be a vampire, specifically Buffy's associate, Angel, and the experience had reaffirmed one of Cordelia's long-held beliefs: better to let the guys do the chasing. She turned to Aura, intending to grant the other girl the benefit of her experienced wisdom. But she was just in time for a rear view, as Aura disappeared into the crowd.

Cordelia sniffed. Some people didn't understand basic courtesy.

The beast leaped down onto Buffy and Angel from the crypt's slanted roof, driving them both to the ground with the force of his fall. The creature snarled as he struck, lashing out with cruel claws. Slayer and vampire alike rolled desperately, barely avoiding the raking swipes. Buffy's weapons bag went flying.

Angel was right, she realized, drawing a stake from her jeans pocket. Something else *always* happened.

She scrambled back to her feet, but Angel acted faster. Even as the beast turned to lunge at him, the vampire struck, stabbing the creature with a savage spearlike strike. He drove the fist of his right hand into his assailant's solar plexus, making the beast double over in pain. The exchange took only a split second, but it gave Buffy a chance to assess the situation.

Their adversary seemed to be some kind of a were-wolf, but like none that she'd seen in any of Giles's books. He had a human frame and build but moved in a low bestial slouch that made his full size difficult to gauge accurately. He had a man's hands, but they were overgrown with thick fur and had hooked, talonlike claws. Human eyes that were clouded with rage stared out from his face, and his features, like his hands, were layered in fur. White froth, liquid and foamy, drooled from a mouth of ragged teeth.

Absurdly, the creature wore denim trousers and a varsity jacket—not in Sunnydale High's red and gold but in colors that Buffy didn't recognize.

"And I thought the penguin was weird," Buffy said softly.

Her words drew the wolf-man's attention. With a low growl he crouched, then sprang. His outstretched hands raced for Buffy's throat.

"Buffy!" Angel said.

She didn't need the warning. She'd already braced herself, her favorite stake poised. When the wolf-man slammed into her, she brought the weapon up, fast and hard. The impact of the beast's lunge was enough to topple her, but not to ruin her aim. The pointed piece of wood stabbed deep into the wolf-man's chest.

Buffy had encountered many varieties of monster since commencing her career as the Slayer. Whether vampire, demon, or zombie, they each had their modes of attack, their specific strengths and weaknesses. One thing, though, was reasonably constant. Heart strikes almost always killed.

This one hadn't.

The quasi-werewolf was on top of her now, pinning her with his weight. His claws found her throat and began to squeeze. From the wolf-man's snarling lips she could feel hot breath against her skin. Buffy's hands found the creature's wrists and she squeezed too. The monster grunted in pain, but his grip didn't falter, not even when she increased the pressure and felt bones grind together.

She felt something else, too, and some corner of her mind duly took note of it. Even as she applied crushing force, she could feel the creature's pulse in her hands, strong and vital.

The thing had a heart, then. Why hadn't the stake done its job? That was a question for later, something to ask Giles. Perhaps he'd favor her with one of his rare direct answers.

The wolf-man's attack had driven the air from her lungs, and she was having difficulty filling them again. Her own pulse pounded in her ears and spots swam before her eyes. The dark night seemed to grow darker. He was trying to kill her, and was doing a reasonably good job.

She gritted her teeth and redoubled her efforts to free herself. The angle made the work awkward, but she struggled to pull the wolf-man's arms apart. The monster's clawed hands shifted, just a bit, and Buffy sucked cool night air greedily. Her vision began to clear.

As the world came back into focus, she saw another pair of hands. Angel's. He reached around from behind and grasped the wolf-man's chin with his left hand, then clamped his right fist atop the brute's head. The vampire forcefully yanked back and up, which made a sound like pottery breaking. Buffy's grasp broke as the beast released his grip on her neck. Angel tore the creature away from her.

"Thanks," she said. She managed a smile. He'd shifted into full vampire mode, the handsome contours of his face morphed into something harsher, but he was still a welcome sight.

"It was my turn," he said. The words came in a rush as he pivoted. Moving with inhuman speed, he slammed the wolf-man against the nearby crypt's marble wall. Before the creature could react, he repeated the action a second and third time. When Angel let go at last, the beast's eyes had closed. For a moment he remained standing, slumped against the wall, and then he slid into an unconscious heap. It was like watching a cartoon.

Buffy pulled herself together and stood, waving aside Angel's offer of help. She gathered up the weapons bag and took hasty inventory. The compact and collapsible crossbow, the bolts, the knives, and the other implements were all there. Only the single stake was missing.

"That's odd," she said.

"Hmm?" Angel asked.

She pointed at their attacker. Even in the shadows her stake was conspicuous. It was buried deep into their assailant's chest, but that chest still rose and fell steadily. Even with a stake in his heart, he was still breathing.

"Shouldn't he be, like, dead?" Buffy asked. "I mean, very dead?"

"I don't know," Angel said. Usually cool and unflappable, he too seemed puzzled now. Warily, he knelt and examined the damaged monster. He sniffed, and shook his head. "He's bleeding," Angel said.

Buffy wondered if the wolf-man's blood tempted Angel, then forced the question from her mind. It seemed rude, somehow.

"Lots of blood," Angel said, musing. He opened the varsity letter jacket. Beneath it was an equally absurd football jersey. It glistened wetly beneath the moon's rays. "Between this and the neck, he should really be dead."

"It's a wooden stake, not silver," Buffy said. Some intuition, vague and half-formed, prompted her to reach again into her weapons bag. "Doesn't it take silver, for werewolves?"

"But this isn't a werewolf," Angel said. He looked up at her again. "I mean, I've met werewolves. They're not hind-leggers. Strictly all fours." He pointed at the night sky. "Besides, it's not the night of the full moon."

"So," the Slayer said, "it's not a werewolf but, rather, an incredible simulation of one."

The conversation had taken on an absurd, other-worldly feel, Buffy realized. She was standing in the moonlight, talking to her more-or-less boyfriend, comparing notes on the operational specifics of werewolves. What had her life come to?

"Whatever he is, he's down for the count," Angel said. He shrugged. "What now?"

"Don't know," Buffy said. With most such encounters, disposing of the evidence wasn't a problem. Vampires collapsed conveniently into dust. Elementals found their, well, element and disappeared. Robots had a welcome tendency to explode and reduce themselves to components that defied easy identification. But a wolf-man, unconscious—

"I don't know how long he can last like this," Angel said, echoing her thoughts.

"Put him out of his misery?" Buffy asked tentatively. She didn't like the idea. It was one thing to slay in battle, but executing an unconscious foe was something else entirely.

"Misery. That's another point," Angel said. Satisfied that their foe was, indeed, out like a light, he turned to face her. "Werewolves are usually victims themselves. They're cursed." The vampire paused, clearly troubled.

Buffy knew why. He had a curse of his own. "Maybe, if we can restrain him, Giles can give us an answer."

"How do we do that?" Angel asked. There were times when he was annoyingly pragmatic. "Do you have anything?"

"Not really," Buffy said. She thought for a moment. She wasn't in the habit of bringing handcuffs on her patrols. "Maybe we can box him up?"

"Where?"

Angel was still kneeling, facing her. She looked past him, at the crypt. "There," she said. "We could come back—"

She noticed the movement just in time. Behind Angel the wolf-man's eyelids fluttered, then opened a split second later. The brute rose to his feet, moving at a startling speed that belied his injuries. Clawed hands neared Angel's throat.

Buffy no longer worried about executing an unconscious foe. The realization came almost as a relief, but then the thought faded and trained reflex took over. Inside the weapons bag, her fingers found the hilt of a *boka,* a bent knife with two razor-sharp curved edges. It was shorter than a machete but better balanced and just as deadly. Buffy hurled the blade without pausing to look, think, or take aim.

The *boka* spun through the moonlit air, passing over Angel's shoulder. Genuine sparks, harsh and electric, flew as the weapon sliced though the wolf-man's neck and dug into the stone beyond.

Heart strikes usually worked. Thus far, at least, outright beheadings *always* did.

"There," she said. "Next time's your turn again."

"I'm not keeping count," the vampire replied, turning to look behind him.

The wolf-man collapsed once more. This time, however, the creature's form slumped forward, caving in on itself. The contours of his remains softened and faded. As they watched, his substance seemed to evaporate, boiling away, first into mist and then into nothingness. In moments, flesh, blood, and clothing alike had all vanished completely. Only Buffy's stake and blade remained.

"Blood's gone," Angel said. He sniffed again. The vampire had a terrifically keen sense of smell, a handy ability, but it wasn't one of his most endearing qualities.

"I can see that," Buffy said. "He cleaned up after himself. And I thought vampires were tidy." Seeing the pained expression on Angel's face, she shrugged. "Sorry," she said meekly. "Nothing personal."

"No, it's not like that," he replied. "It's the blood. The blood scent should last for hours at the very least, but it's gone already." He retrieved her weapons and handed them to her. The blade was chipped where it had struck stone, but both instruments were spotlessly clean. "What was on these and in the air is gone," Angel continued. "There's no residue at all. It's like he was never here."

"The bruises on my neck say different," Buffy said, but without any particular concern. Slayers healed fast. "He wasn't a werewolf, then?"

"I don't know what he was," Angel replied.

"Definitely one for the books, then," Buffy said. "Giles's books, that is."

Angel nodded in agreement. He knelt to study the soil where the wolf-man had fallen. The surrounding grass was bent and disturbed but perfectly dry. Angel seemed fascinated by the phenomenon of blood that could disappear without a trace. Buffy put it down to professional interest.

She put the *boka* back in her bag where it belonged, but kept a secure grip on the stake. The night was still young, after all.

The band was just about to start its second set when Aura made her escape. Cordelia was a dear with a fashion sense to die for, but even Aura found some of her guidance overbearing—especially when it came to guys. Harmony Kendall might hang on Cordy's every word, but not Aura. The Queen of Sunnydale High was a fine role model and companion, but Aura didn't need a second mother. When she saw Cordelia's features compose themselves into the familiar expression that promised a lecture, she rose without comment. She wiggled the fingers of her left hand in a parting gesture. Harmony noticed and waved back. Cordelia, focused intently on the world beyond their shared table, didn't seem to notice.

She never did, as far as Aura could tell. Cordy thought that it was her world, and everyone else just lived in it.

The Bronze was hopping, at least by weeknight standards. The table area and dance floor were crowded enough to make Aura's path zig and zag as she threaded through the other patrons. Most of them were familiar. A few times she paused to exchange niceties with other high school girls who weren't as pretty or as smart as she was. College girls were another matter; Aura eyed them warily, and they did the same to her. Aura knew that she was beautiful, and so did they, but competition was ugly.

She was looking for the sleepy-eyed stranger. Aura didn't care much for biker types, but something about this guy appealed to her, and she wanted to address the issue. Neither of her tablemates seemed poised to compete. Cordelia wasn't very quick on the draw lately; Aura had begun to wonder if she was seeing someone. And Harmony was sticking to the Queen of Sunnydale High like a blond shadow. But there were other girls aplenty in the Bronze tonight, and Aura didn't see any reason to let them have a chance.

The band started its second set as she glided past the bar. TDQYDJP was soon into a bluesy-salsa-reggae thing about good love gone wrong. In a world full of pairs, Aura's target stood at the dance floor's edge with his back to her.

"Hey!" she said, tapping his shoulder. Her prod met with pleasing resistance. Aura liked hard muscle.

He turned. Up close he looked even better. His eyes had a mesmerizing intensity. They burned, half-hidden beneath drooping lids.

"Yeah?" the guy asked. It was less a word than a questioning grunt, but Aura didn't mind. She'd never been much for conversation.

"Looking for someone?" she asked. She smiled up at him.

"Yeah," the guy said. This time the grunt sounded a bit like "yes."

"Good," Aura said, her smile widening. "*I'm* someone."

And then they were off, their bodies moving in perfect rhythm.

Aura felt as if they'd taken flight together. The world seemed to fall away, and the throbbing beat carried them along, a perfect matching pair. Like two leaves on the wind, they swept across the dance floor, turning and spinning and spiraling in wild abandon.

She was making a bit of a spectacle of herself, she knew. Aura accepted her beauty as a fact of life, and knew she looked good in motion. Some corner of her mind noticed that other Bronze patrons were watching them, and noted their expressions. The guys were properly enthusiastic or amused; generally speaking, the girls seemed envious or scandalized. Aura didn't care. The night was young and so was she; the rest of the world could go to hell.

Their track carried them back to the dance floor's edge. The music faded as the band ended its first song and started the next. Aura took advantage of the moment to pause and catch her breath.

"Wow!" she said.

He smiled. Broad, sensuous lips pulled back over his movie-star teeth as he leaned in close. He didn't say anything, but words didn't seem very important just then.

"Yeah," Aura said, still drawing the club's smoky air into herself. As if of its own accord, her head titled back a bit, presenting her half-open mouth. She closed her eyes, readying herself for his kiss.

It never came.

After a too-long moment, Aura's eyes opened, darting from side to side in dismay. She was alone—not absolutely alone, but alone in a crowd. The dance floor was still crowded, but the only person who really mattered to Aura was gone. Her partner had vanished without a trace. She flushed in confusion and embarrassment and more than a little anger.

Ditched. She'd *never* been ditched before. It defied reason.

Standing nearby was another couple, the purple-haired girl and the bald fatty, who had evidently made their peace. The next song started, low and slow, and they moved out onto the dance floor again. Aura saw the girl shoot her a puzzled glance.

"Hey!" Aura said to her. The Goth was college age or older, and she certainly didn't look like anyone Aura wanted to meet, but that didn't matter right now. "Hey, you! Did you see where my partner went?"

"No," the purple-haired girl said over her date's shoulder. Her lips were black. "It was weird," she said, speaking loud in order to be heard over the band's increasing sound. "He, like, faded away or something."

Chapter Three

Xander knew his school and its between-class traffic patterns well. In nice weather, like today, most students cut through Sunnydale High's central courtyard whenever possible. The courtyard route not only made the trip between school wings shorter, but it was also a nice change from the hallways' fluorescent lighting and institutional paint scheme. Xander too liked the moments of fresh air and sunshine.

Seconds after the school bell rang, he was standing outside with his back to one brick wall, about ten feet outside the entrance that led to the cafeteria. The surrounding courtyard sported little islands of landscaped greenery bounded by retaining walls, which served as impromptu gathering places. At this time of day they were empty. Xander purposely ignored the courtyard's bulletin board kiosk, the official posting place for announcements. He wanted his message received and read, not buried under other postings about garage sales, play tryouts, and policy changes.

"Here you go," Xander said as a sizeable segment of the student body surged past. He handed out the orange-paper flyers as rapidly as he could. "Check it out. Something you will enjoy!"

He knew almost everyone's name but personally greeted only a few. He was there to pass out paper, not to make conversation, after all. If he tried to make things personal, with a greeting or even a nod of recognition, he was just giving the lucky guy or gal a chance to say no. But if he refrained even from making eye contact, there was a mighty good chance that the sheet of paper would leave his hand and find a new one. Speed was the secret.

"Take a look," Xander said. "Tell your friends."

Erik Morrison from the wrestling team accepted the flyer without even seeming to notice that it had been offered, then he wadded it into a ball and let it fall to the walkway. Ralph Ellis, who'd been trying to recruit Xander for forensics competition, took one and tucked it in a pocket. Willow accepted one with a smile, then asked for more and tried to start a conversation before deciding that she really, really had to get to her next class because she hated being late. Jonathan Levenson accepted his without comment, but Jonathan never really said very much, anyway. Harmony Kendall reached for one reflexively, then recoiled in horror when she realized that it was an offering from Xander. A teacher he didn't recognize— a substitute?—just shook her head in rejection and rolled her eyes. John Garcia took three, grabbing them up as if they were some kind of prize.

Friend, foe, and stranger alike, the tide of humanity moved on. In the five or so minutes when traffic was enough to make tarrying worthwhile, Xander managed to spread the good word about the drive-in festival to more than a hundred students. He'd need to get more flyers from his locker before trying again.

"Harris," said a familiar and disliked voice. "Just what do you think you're doing?"

Principal Snyder approached. He was a little man with ratlike features. The current joke about Snyder was that he had a face only a mother could love, but even his mother wasn't sure.

"Hello, Mr. Snyder, sir," Xander said. He came to attention, which was probably a mistake. It only made Snyder seem shorter. "Just—"

Snyder snatched one of the flyers. He read it quickly, or at least enough of it to know what he held. His narrow lips curved in an uneasy approximation of a smile. "A drive-in?" he asked. "In this day and age?"

Xander nodded. He hoped the confrontation would be brief; the between-class break was nearly over. "Yes, sir, Mr. Snyder, sir," he said, feeling terribly alone. Most of the other students had made themselves scarce.

"Huh," Snyder said, returning his attention to the handbill. Finally, grudgingly, he nodded. "This is advertising," he said. "I shouldn't let you do this on school grounds."

Xander swallowed nervously. In his mind's eye he saw a house of cards collapse and a small bag with a dollar sign on its side sprout wings and fly away.

Snyder folded the sheet of paper neatly and slid it into his jacket pocket. "Go ahead," he said. "Just clean up after yourself. I don't like litter, Harris."

"Th-thank you, sir!" Xander said, relieved and surprised. Snyder never cut anyone any slack.

"I mean it. I'm holding you personally responsible," the rat-man said, then turned on one heel and strode away as Xander watched in disbelief.

Snyder had smiled. Snyder had actually smiled. That kind of thing just didn't happen. Clearly, the world had gone nuts.

"Whoops," Buffy said as her fingertips grazed her drink can. Even the glancing contact was enough to topple the container, and before she could right it, thick droplets of pink protein drink splashed from its open top. "Sorry."

"Buffy! Please!" Giles said.

Six massive books lay on the library table before her and Willow, each bound in what she sincerely hoped was leather. A rivulet of protein drink flowed toward one. The half dozen volumes weren't from the school's state-issued collection, but from Giles's assets. With the protective instinct of a mother hen, he slid the endangered tome aside with one hand while he blotted the spilled drink with a handkerchief held in the other.

"I said I was sorry," Buffy said. She was, too, but

not sorry enough to forego her liquid lunch. Slaying burned a lot of calories.

"Yes, I can tell you're quite distraught," Giles said.

"See anything familiar yet, Buffy?" Willow asked, obviously eager to change the subject.

"Nope," the Slayer said. She shook her head emphatically and pointed at each of the books in turn. "No. Uh-uh. Nopers. That's a negatory, good buddy." With each rejection, she pointed at a different volume using the same hand that held her drink.

"Please, Buffy, if I could trouble you to be careful with your beverage," Giles said. He seemed physically uncomfortable. "That copy of the *Crimson Chronicles* is more than six hundred years old. It would be terribly difficult to replace."

She pulled the drink back, so that it was no longer above the open tome. Just in time, too; a drop of condensation trickled down its side and fell to the floor. "O-*kay*," Buffy said. "But just because you ask so nice."

Giles had opened the half-dozen books, presenting illustrations for her review. The pictures varied wildly in style and execution, but each was of a wolf or wolflike creature. Some sported horns or forked tails or human eyes. One picture was an unsettling fusion of a human head and a wolf's body, precisely the opposite of what Buffy was looking for. Only the sixth image was even a slight match.

"This guy's in the neighborhood," Buffy said, pointing at the last open book.

Giles and Willow looked. The image she'd indicated was of a human figure with a canine head. The anonymous artist had rendered the portrait in awkward profile but with nice detail. The subject was bare-chested, was dressed in sandals and a loincloth, and carried a staff in one very human-looking hand.

"That's not a werewolf," Willow said. She sounded faintly dismayed. "That's Anubis, the god of the dead in ancient Egypt." When Giles and Buffy both looked at her in surprise, she continued more defensively, "Hey, I've been reading up on this stuff! I'm not just a Net geek!"

Giles lifted the open book. He made a great production of reading from the crabbed lettering. "It's an image of Anpu, actually," he said.

Willow rolled her eyes slightly. She said, "And Anpu is another name for . . . ?"

Giles sighed. "Anubis."

"It doesn't matter," Buffy said. "I don't care if it's Anubis or Andrew—"

"Anpu," Giles said softly.

"—or Anpu. That guy's not who I saw last night. He's just in the same general neighborhood," Buffy continued impatiently. "Human body with added wolfy badness."

"Anubis is a jackal deity, not wolf," Willow said.

"I. Don't. Care," Buffy said, emphasizing each word. "I want to know what he's doing in Sunnydale." She drained the last of her shake and thought back to wolf-man's absurd attire. "And I'd like to know what team he's playing for too, if that's not too much trouble."

Giles hadn't entirely believed her when she'd made her preliminary report. Convincing him proved difficult. Her story just felt too far outside his personal experience and research. He'd listened to her account of the evening's patrol but had actually tried to correct her on the details, which was ridiculous. While Buffy was prowling the cemetery and not kissing Angel, Giles must have been home sipping tea and watching BBC satellite feeds, or whatever it was he did with his evenings. That didn't seem to matter to Giles, though, not even when the Slayer pointed it out to him. Again and again he asked her if she was certain the wolf-man hadn't attacked her on all fours, or if she were sure that she hadn't used a silver bullet, or if the autumn moon might not actually have been full.

"I have some other texts," Giles said slowly, closing the Anubis book with great reluctance. "One in particular might be of use. We can consult it later."

"Later?" Willow asked. "Now is better, isn't it?"

"But I can't seem to find it at the moment."

That was a surprise. The Watcher was obsessively orderly. Not only did his books run according to a strict filing system that only he fully understood, but he kept his pens and pencils sorted according to type, color, age, and size. Both girls looked at him in plain disbelief.

"I'm certain it's just mis-shelved," Giles said.

"You never mis-shelve things, Giles," Buffy said incredulously.

He shook his head. "Not by me, then. Someone decided to explore the stacks earlier," Giles said. "Someone untidy."

"I thought the whole idea of your working on-site

here was that you could keep your books in the library and no one would screw with them," Buffy said. "Hide in plain sight and all that. I mean, we're the only students who hang out here, right?"

"It wasn't a student," Giles replied. He looked even more uncomfortable.

"Oh? Spill!" Buffy said.

"Yes, Giles, make with the spillage," Willow agreed. "There's new faculty?"

"It would appear that the school secured the services of a new nurse," Giles said. He gathered up the other volumes and set them on a cart for re-shelving. "I came upon her in the stacks. She was making herself at home and appears to have done some . . . rearranging."

"A new nurse?" Buffy asked. In a more ominous tone, she continued, "The name's not Ratchet, is it?"

"No, no, not at all. Her name is Inga."

"Inga?" Willow asked.

"She's . . . Swedish," Giles said. The words came very slowly.

"Uh-huh," Buffy said. "Nurse Inga." She raised both hands and made beckoning motions for him to be more forthcoming. "Swedish and . . ."

"Swedish and very attractive," Giles said. He cleared his throat and loosened his collar. "Blue-eyed and blond, quite tall, and very, um—"

"Giles!" Buffy said. She stamped her feet in delight. She always liked catching him in a human moment. "You *dog*! You sly, sly dog!"

"That's uncalled for," Giles said.

"Hallo, mister library man," Buffy said in her best

bad Swedish accent. "Do you speak the Svensk?"

"Zee Alps, zey are very nice zis time of year!" Willow said, following suit. "Ve could go exploring, yah?" Her accent was even worse.

"No!" Giles said, clearly flustered. "It was nothing like that! I found her poking about and tried to direct her attentions elsewhere!"

Buffy planted her elbow and rested her chin on her hand, looking up at him. "I bet you did," she said, in tones that were soft and knowing. At her side Willow giggled.

"There's no way I can win this, is there?" Giles asked.

"Nope. None."

"Ahem," Giles said, and soldiered on. "Very well, then. She made a bit of a mess." He paused. "I was just re-ordering things when you two arrived, but—"

"Is anything missing?" Willow asked anxiously. "Some of your books are bad mojo."

"I'm not sure just yet, but I'm beginning to think so," Giles confessed. "Inga left empty-handed, though. That's why I wasn't particularly concerned until you asked for all my, um, 'werewolf goodies.'"

Buffy grinned. Her liquid lunch was done now and she dropped the empty can in a nearby wastepaper basket. Metal hit metal with a *clang* much too loud for the library's quiet confines. "Dashed inconvenient, that!" the Slayer said. She'd shifted to faux British. "Can me and the little miss give you a hand, guv'nor?"

Giles seemed to shudder. "I rather think not," he said.

"What happens if you can't find it?" Buffy asked. "Can I interrogate the nurse? Please, please?"

"I've got some questions for her," Willow said eagerly. "The hussy!"

"Please," Giles said. He put one hand to his forehead, massaging his temples as he shaded his eyes. "Oh, please. Let me do what I can first. And if I can't find it—"

Both Buffy and Willow looked at him brightly. They were eager to commence their investigation.

"If I can't find it by the end of the school day, we'll revisit the matter," Giles said. "I have some other works at home that may be of service. I'll review them this evening. Contact me before you go on patrol."

The sun was high in the midday sky, but the walls of Angel's lair sheltered him from its heat and menacing rays. He bolted the door against unwanted intrusion and dimmed the lights almost to the point of darkness, creating a private world of cool gloom. Alone with his thoughts, Angel lay on the bed and stared at the ceiling. Soon he was neither asleep nor awake, but in a tranquil state somewhere in between. Images and sensory impressions flitted though his mind like fish in the sea, each one bright and distinct and unique.

Being a vampire had its advantages. His enormous strength and stamina were beyond a human's dreams. He experienced the world through heightened senses. He could hide his thoughts from mind readers, and his image was invisible to mirrors. These were among the gifts of vampirism.

No.

They weren't gifts, not really. They were symptoms, part and parcel of his current state, like his thirst for blood or his vulnerability to direct sunlight. He would forfeit them all, strengths and weaknesses alike, for the chance to be human again. Even so, there was no denying that the traits of vampirism had their uses.

One of his most useful attributes was an eidetic memory, the ability to recall experiences in full quality and detail. Buffy called it "photographic," but the word was misleading. It was more than that, much more.

For Angel, with a bit of effort, the past could be as real as the present. Sight and sound, smell and taste, even touch—his mind recorded them in exacting fidelity. Angel had walked the world for nearly two and a half centuries, and he remembered clearly almost every moment of his existence.

Just now he recalled the events of the previous evening. The night was cool, the moon half-full. Crickets chirped and leaves rustled. Angel had been standing silently beneath a tree in the cemetery. He'd been alone, but was waiting to hear the familiar footsteps and heartbeat.

He slowly replayed the entire sequence of events in his mind. He walked again through the autumn night and heard anew the words he'd exchanged in low tones with Buffy. Once more he felt her breath on his cool skin. Then the wolf-man fell on them from above, and the battle began.

He considered the entire scene again and again. Like a dog might gnaw, he mulled over the memories, striving to extract every iota of information they held. Something about the night's adventure troubled him, even now. He had to know why.

The battle was nothing special, really; there'd been dozens others like it. Recover from an enemy's attack, then counterattack. Defend Buffy and be defended by her, in turn. Triumph. The previous evening was like many before it, and like countless others to come.

Only one thing was unique: the monster himself. Angel was certain he'd seen the creature before, or one like it, but the memory was a faint one. Tantalizing and elusive, it hung at the very threshold of his ability to recall, defying his cognitive abilities. If he'd seen the wolf-man before, the encounter must have been a fleeting one, too brief and inconsequential to register in a vampire's memory. He might not have even seen the creature itself, he slowly realized; he might only have seen an image of the thing, a painting or drawing or photograph. . . .

When recognition came, it struck like a thunderbolt. Angel's eyes widened in surprise and his entire body tensed. He bolted upright in bed and shook his head in disbelief.

"No," he said softly. "That's ridiculous."

Buffy spun the dial and lifted the hasp. The mechanism made a *ka-chunk* sound, and her locker door swung open. She inspected its slightly chaotic interior. It held mostly teenage girly stuff; she didn't keep much Slayer paraphernalia at school, choosing to rely on Giles's resources instead. Dropping off two textbooks, she picked up a third, then used the mounted door mirror to make a quick hair-and-lipstick check. Everything was in order.

The walk from her fifth-period class to her sixth-period one typically took two minutes. Granted a five minute break, she had enough time to make a stop along the way. She smiled impishly. There was more than one kind of reconnaissance patrol.

"Knock, knock!" Buffy said a moment later, air-rapping her knuckles on the open door to the school nurse's station. "Hello? Anyone here?"

"Just a moment, dear!" came a woman's voice from the examination area. The privacy curtain whisked aside and a woman wearing a white uniform appeared. She was short and middle-aged and had curly brown hair that came from a perm and a dye bottle. Her smile was warm and friendly. "Why, Buffy Summers!" the woman said. She spoke with a musical Wisconsin lilt. "You never come calling. Is something wrong?"

"Nurse Forman?" Buffy asked, utterly nonplussed.

"Why, yes, dearie," she chirped. "You sound disappointed."

"Um, no, no, not at all," Buffy said. "Just surprised." She had expected to be greeted by the Norse goddess Giles had so reluctantly described.

The attending nurse cocked an eyebrow at her, and Buffy felt briefly ashamed of herself. Kitty Forman was motherly and sweet, with an endearing pixie-ish quality. Buffy knew that she should have been happy to see the familiar woman. "It's just—I heard there was a new nurse, and I wanted to meet and greet," Buffy continued. Even to her own ears the words sounded lame.

"New nurse? Was her name Ursula?" Forman asked.

"Inga," Buffy corrected.

Forman shook her head and laughed, a sound like silver bells. "No Inga here," she said. "Or Ursula, for that matter."

"But—"

"People have been asking about this Ursula or Inga or whoever person all day," Nurse Forman said. "I don't know what the world's coming to. Someone must be playing a prank." She shook her head. "A cruel, cruel prank."

Buffy wasn't so sure. Giles was a hard man to fool. If he'd seen a Valkyrie in the library, there'd *been* a Valkyrie in the library.

A chime rang. Nurse Forman waved Buffy toward the hallway. "There's the warning bell," she said. "You'd better scat! Don't want to be late for class, dear!"

Chapter Four

The afternoon sun was bright. Cordelia lingered on one of the low retaining walls in the high school courtyard and luxuriated in the warmth. She needed a chance to unwind, and this was as good a place as any. There was a half-hour gap between the end of her classes and the beginning of cheerleading practice, and Cordelia intended to make the most of it. She tilted her head back, closed her eyes, and breathed deeply. The autumn air was scented with green, thanks to the ongoing work of the landscaping crew. The moment was worth savoring. It was like an afternoon at the day spa, except it was free, so it couldn't be as good.

A shadow fell across her and lingered. Someone was blocking her sun. And she had a pretty good guess who it must be.

"Go away, you," she said, without lifting her eyelids. "I'm busy."

"Good. I'd like to get busy too. Think you can help me with that?"

She was right. The voice was Xander's, filled with an easy familiarity that she found a bit presumptuous, even now. It was one thing to neck with a guy in a broom closet while vampires swarmed the hallways outside, and quite another to let him act like you were part of his life.

"Go away," she said again, but more gently this time, and with open eyes. Classes were done and witnesses were unlikely, so she favored him with a smile. It was brief but genuine.

"What's the matter, Cordy?" he asked, as he stepped aside. "Not ready to be seen in public with me just yet?"

"'Just yet'?" She quoted his words back to him, but with a bit of a bantering tone. She didn't want them to sting too badly. "That implies ever."

She'd never tell anyone, but Cordelia had decided that there was a bit of long-term promise in the Harris boy. Xander's typical teen gawkiness was fading fast, and if he wasn't yet handsome, he had strong features and a good smile. Now that she'd gotten to know him better, much to her own surprise, she'd found that he could be sweet and warm.

Not that Cordelia spent much time telling him so.

"On your way to work?" she asked. She crossed her long legs. They were clad in designer jeans that fit like paint, and Xander's eyes followed the movement. Good. It was always good to know that a guy was still interested. More than once, it had seemed to Cordelia that Xander was on the brink of taking her for granted. She couldn't allow that to happen, no matter how weird it seemed to be with him.

"Huh? Oh, yeah," he said, looking up again. His right hand held a thick sheaf of the orange handbills he'd been handing out to anybody who would take one. In his left hand was a staple gun. "Boss-man asked me to post some around town and stir up some interest among today's troubled teens."

"Seems kind of low-tech," Cordelia said.

"Boss-man's a bit low-tech himself," Xander replied. "What can I say? He likes the old ways."

Cordelia shrugged. She couldn't think of a response worth making.

Xander could, or thought he could. "You should check it out, Cordy," he said. "You'd have fun." He paused. "*We'd* have fun," he amended.

"You're still on that?" Cordelia asked. Without trying to be subtle about it, she looked at her wristwatch, a sterling silver wafer that her father had given her. Fifteen minutes had passed. She would need to report for drills soon.

Xander's answer was a silent nod.

"*Mysteries of Chainsaw Mansion*? Please." Cordelia grimaced. "Find someone else," she said. "Someone who's not a girl."

"Not even Willow?" Xander said.

"Especially not Willow," Cordelia said. "But especially, especially not me. I plan to be busy."

"Busy?" Xander sounded anxious. "Busy with someone? Someone else?"

"Not like that," Cordelia said, taking pity. "I'll likely be at the Bronze, watching Aura make a fool of herself again."

Without being invited or authorized, Xander sat down beside her. Cordelia decided to let it slide; after all, the courtyard was largely deserted. "Aura?" he said. "Fool? Again? It's sharing time."

Cordelia took a deep breath. There was that endearing goofiness again. She told Xander about the previous evening. Quickly she recounted her friend's sudden fascination with the mysterious stranger and how disappointed Aura had been when she returned to the table.

"He disappeared?" Xander asked. He listened to her attentively, which was always gratifying.

"That's what Aura said," Cordelia said. She corrected herself. "I mean, that's what Aura said the Goth girl said. I didn't see it myself."

Cordelia's world had been a reasonably clear-cut place before the weirdness that she associated with Buffy Summers had started to nibble at its edges.

"That can't be good," Xander said. "The disappearing thing, I mean."

"Guys have bailed on Aura before," Cordelia said. She looked at her watch. Another five minutes had passed.

"Bailed, not disappeared," Xander pointed out.

"That's if you trust someone with purple hair to get things right," Cordelia said tartly.

"A mysterious stranger disappears mysteriously in a town filled with mystery right on top of the

Hellmouth? And you say there's no mystery about it?" Xander teased.

Cordelia rolled her eyes. She knew what his next words would be.

"Have you talked to Buffy about this?" he asked.

"No," she replied testily.

"I really think—"

"It wasn't like that," she said, interrupting. Her tone was sharper now. "I *told* you, Xander, guys have bailed on Aura before."

They sat together in a tense moment of silence. She was sure that Xander knew he'd erred. He had to. She'd told him enough times that invoking other girls to her wasn't a very good idea. Cordelia might get along with Buffy these days, but that didn't mean she wanted Xander to keep bringing up her name.

"I've seen some strangers in my day," he said finally, in a musing tone.

"I'm sure you have," she replied.

He surprised her then. "I'm sorry," he said, changing the subject.

"Huh?" Cordelia asked, genuinely startled by his two words. Xander didn't apologize very often. Usually he just protested that the world in general and women in particular didn't make any sense. Then he would either storm off until the smoke settled or stay and try to wisecrack his way out of the situation. Either way, life would go on. It seemed out of character for him to apologize, especially so promptly and for such a minor slight.

"The Buffy thing," he said again. "I shouldn't tell

you what to do." He shrugged. "I'm just a typical teenage boy and I make mistakes. I really am sorry."

Was he sorry that he'd brought up her name? Or was he just sorry that he'd suggested she report to Buffy, like some kind of flunky or minion? Either option seemed equally likely, so Cordelia gave him the benefit of the doubt.

"That's okay," she said. "No biggie."

This time the shared silence was more comfortable. Though still relieved that they didn't have an audience, Cordelia found she didn't mind his company. For a second she actually considered going to the stupid drive-in with him.

But only for a second.

"Cordy?" Xander said slowly. "If they changed the school colors, I'd hear about it, wouldn't I? I mean, I'd *know,* right?" He sounded even more confused than usual.

She blinked again in surprise. The question came out of nowhere. "They haven't changed the colors, Xander," she said with forced patience. "I should know. They just issued new uniforms, for the team and the squad. Why are you so interested in fashion?"

His answer was to point to the far end of the courtyard. A girl lounged in a shadowed fire exit. She seemed to be looking in their direction.

"That's why," Xander said.

At first Cordelia thought that he'd been dumb enough to raise the issue of another woman again. Then she realized that he was trying to make another point.

Xander's finger-point morphed into a hand wave. "Hi, there!" he said, a bit more loudly. The girl made no response.

Tall and curvy, she wasn't a member of the student body; Cordelia was certain of that. She kept tabs on the competition and knew her rivals by sight, even at a distance. The stranger wasn't a fellow student.

That wasn't the only thing wrong. The girl wore a cheerleading uniform. It was a cut different from Cordelia's, passé and unattractive, with a too-long skirt that did nothing for the poor thing's legs. The style of the jersey was wrong too, but that wasn't even the worst of it.

"Pink and white?" Cordelia asked, appalled. "Who wears pink and white?"

Xander shrugged. "Mary Kay Academy?" he asked. "Dixieland High? Peppermint Secondary?"

Cordelia sprang to her feet to investigate. She hardly noticed that Xander did the same. This was a matter of competition and territory, serious business for a person with Cordelia's social prominence.

"Hey! Hey, you!" she called. Her words carried the length of the nearly deserted courtyard and echoed from the surrounding walls. The girl came to sudden attention, startled.

The distance from the retaining wall to the mystery cheerleader was perhaps twenty yards. Cordelia didn't bother to run, but she strode briskly enough that the distance dwindled rapidly. "I want to talk to you!" she said loudly.

Xander kept pace. "Cordy," he said, at her side, "is

this really a good idea? I mean, I like a catfight as much as the next guy—"

"Hush," she told him. Boys could be so stupid.

Closer now, she could see the other girl better. The pink and white outfit wasn't the least of the stranger's offenses against good taste. She was blond, like Buffy, but wore her hair in a frizzy cloud that was years out of date and absolutely impractical for cheerleading work. Her makeup was wrong too, florid tones applied without blending or style. Cordelia wasn't very good with specific dates, but she knew passé when she saw it, and she was seeing it now.

What was the girl thinking?

"Okay, lady," Cordelia said, a mere ten steps away now. "You and me, we need to—*Hey!*"

The girl turned. She opened the door and darted through it, entering the school's interior without a backward glance. The door slammed shut behind her.

Cordelia and Xander quickly followed her inside, but she was nowhere to be seen. The locker-lined halls were completely empty. Not even distant telltale footsteps could be heard. The strange girl had simply disappeared.

"Well," Xander said. He looked completely baffled.

"Yeah, well," Cordelia agreed. Finally, reluctantly, she said what she knew he had to be thinking. "I guess I'd better have that chat with Buffy after all."

Willow's room was homier than Buffy's. Maybe it was because she spent more time at home and gave it a more lived-in look. Maybe it was just because the

Rosenbergs had lived at their address in Sunnydale for so long. Tastefully decorated and tidy, this was actually Willow's home, in a way that the Summers house still wasn't Buffy's. The Slayer was still a new girl in town, relatively speaking, but Willow had lived in town all her life. She had roots here, and not in a gross, monster-plant kind of way.

Of course, some of these roots were newer than others. Willow's laptop had a very nice wireless modem that could take her online almost instantly, no matter where she was. Her home setup with high-speed fiber-optic cables was even better.

Buffy, perched on the edge of Willow's neatly made bed, felt utterly out of her league as the other girl's hands moved along the keyboard. They looked like tangoing spiders. Buffy stared at the monitor the same way Xander stared at girls: with complete fascination and focus. The keys seemed barely able to keep up with Willow's fingertips. Buffy understood just enough of what she was doing to realize that Willow had a genius for manipulating search engines, guessing passwords, and cracking encryption. The Internet world was Willow's oyster, even if she didn't eat shellfish.

The computer's speakers came to life, emitting demonic laughter, that then resolved itself into Latin-sounding phrases. Willow had set the volume very low, so that her parents wouldn't hear, but the effect still startled. The monitor screen, which Buffy could see over her friend's shoulder, filled with dancing skeletons. They were electric blue against a field of flames.

"I don't think that's what we want," Buffy said warily. "At least, I hope it's not."

"I don't think so either," Willow said. She studied her find. "What's 'German Dungeon Rock'?" she asked. "This guy really, really likes it."

"Don't know," Buffy said. "Don't want to." She picked up one of the stuffed animals that were part of Willow's room decor. She gazed into the stuffed bear's black button eyes. It seemed like a very long time since she'd had stuffed animals of her own, a long time and a world away. Part of her still missed them, though, especially Mr. Gordo, her beloved stuffed pig.

Willow entered some more commands. The skeletons faded away.

"Did you tell Giles about the nurse?" Willow asked without missing a keystroke, her eyes fixated on the screen. Her computer expertise extended to multitasking proficiency.

"Yeah," Buffy said. "He didn't quite believe me."

"Huh?" Willow said, surprised.

More than one of her previous reports had been met with initial skepticism. Willow and Xander might accept Buffy's word as gospel. Even Cordelia, when pressed, might grant that the Slayer had a certain subject-matter expertise. But Giles could be a tougher nut to crack. Buffy told Willow how after her visit to the nurse's station she made a return to the library to tell Giles that Kitty Forman remained comfortably installed in the school administration. The only reasonable conclusion was that Inga had been a ringer and was probably up to no good. Giles said she might have been interviewing or maybe a temp of some sort. He promised to ask Principal Snyder.

"Well, it wasn't that bad," Buffy said. "It's not like she was a *giant* nurse with fangs or anything."

"He just wants to explore the Alps with Inga," Willow said, in a slight echo of her earlier bad accent. She continued typing.

"Ya," Buffy said, then set aside the toy bear. "Any luck?"

A pinky finger hit enter one final time. One last report filled the screen. Willow shook her head.

"Bubkes," she said, turning in her chair to face Buffy. "Same as with Giles's books. No hits of note on 'Sunnydale' plus 'drive-in' plus various hot-topic terms like 'mysterious death' or 'sacrifice' or 'brain weevil.' Drop 'drive-in' from the query string and hundreds of matches come up, running back centuries—"

"Well, the Hellmouth has been here a long time," Buffy said, interrupting.

"But 'drive-in' seems to be what you'd call an exclusionary criterion," Willow said. The specialized words sounded a trifle odd coming from her; she usually just worked her computer magic without explaining how it worked. "It's right at the edge of the mouth too. The land might be clean."

"Huh," Buffy said, thinking. Outside, the sun had begun to set. She needed to leave soon. "That would be a nice change."

"Did your mom say anything else about the place?" Willow asked.

"Nope," Buffy said. "Some friend of hers said the

place has a 'history of trouble.' Hereabouts that means someone got turned inside out or something."

"Not this time," Willow said. "I even accessed the crime reports. Not nothing at all, but nothing of note." She paused. "You're worried about Xander?"

"Not worried," Buffy said. "Concerned, maybe. The boy does have a history."

That was putting it lightly. For a civilian, even a civilian who ran with the Slayer, Xander had proved to be a lightning rod for trouble. Again and again the amiable teenager found himself up to his neck in the bad stuff, typically through no fault of his own.

Well, through *little* fault of his own, at least.

"Have you talked?" Willow asked. She closed out her search engines and pulled up a word processor instead. Homework was pending.

"No," Buffy said slowly. "I don't want to, unless there's more to go on. And I don't want him getting the wrong idea. He's hell-bent on going to the movies, though." According to the ubiquitous handbills and Xander's eager accounts, the next night was the drive-in's grand reopening.

"You could go with him!" Willow said. "Keep an eye out!"

Buffy shook her head. "C'mon, Willow," she said. "I'd have to miss patrol. Besides, I don't want to give him the wrong idea."

Xander's attraction to Buffy had long since become a given in her life, and she didn't stop often to think about it. He was a good guy, and she trusted him with her life. Even so, there didn't seem to be much point in adding fuel to the fire. Alone with Xander, at the drive-in . . .

"I meant we could both go with him," Willow said, a bit plaintively. "*I* don't mind giving him the wrong idea."

"C'mon, Will," Buffy said. "Those things don't work that way."

"Don't worry about it, then," Willow said reluctantly. She toyed with her computer's mouse. "He'll be fine without me—um, without us." She had known Xander Harris all her life. Alhough the two girls rarely talked about it, Buffy was quite aware that Willow had a bit of a crush on her childhood chum. "He's tough. I'd be more fretful about this Inga character."

"Huh?" Buffy asked. Her weapons bag sat on the floor, next to her sensibly shod feet. She picked it up and glanced at the contents. She was carrying more blades than usual tonight. Better safe than sorry.

"Mysterious stranger plus missing book," Willow pointed out. "That can't be good news."

"Willow, she's a nurse," Buffy said, tossing her hair for emphasis.

"Nurses have needles!"

"I've got some kind of a werewolf to worry about. Werewolves are bad news," Buffy said. "If this even *is* a werewolf."

"I guess so," Willow said. "But I've met a scary nurse or two in my day, and there's still the missing book thing."

"Giles has plenty of books," Buffy said. She knew that Willow was right, but her mind was already on patrol. The nurse impostor was a mystery but not a pressing problem, at least not right now.

"Did you know Giles belongs to the Grimoire of the Month Club?"

"Can't say it surprises me," Buffy said. She shouldered her bag. "The wolves will be howling soon."

"I hope you're wrong about that," Willow said.

Buffy hoped so too.

Xander was working the blocks that flanked the east side of Main Street. It was a reasonably well-off and trafficked section of town, where franchises of national retail chains rubbed shoulders with locally owned restaurants, galleries, and shops. This was pretty far from Xander's usual haunts—no fast-food joints here—but today it worked well for him. Many of the men and women standing sentry behind cash registers were local entrepreneurs, ready to lend a sympathetic ear to his pitch.

"Thanks a million, Mr. Tate," he said to the man behind the soda fountain ice cream counter. "I really appreciate it."

"Hey, what's good for local business is good for me," Tate said. He was heavyset and completely bald. A spotless white apron was stretched tight across his sizeable stomach. He'd manned the old-fashioned soda fountain for as long as Xander could remember. "You'll have to make your own space, though," Tate said.

Xander took hasty inventory of the community bulletin board next to the corner pay phone. The cork tiles were layered thick with postings. Moving quickly, he peeled away a dozen outdated band announcements, sales brochures, and missing-pet announcements. He wondered briefly if people in other towns lost as many dogs and cats, or if it was just part of life on the Hellmouth. Then he shook his head. There were happier things to think about.

Once he'd cleared enough space, and a healthy margin beyond, he positioned one of his handbills and stapled it in place. He wadded up the discarded documents and dropped them in a wastebasket.

"There," he said, making a great show of clapping his hands together as if to clean them. "A job well done is its own reward."

"Yeah, well, good luck to you all," Tate said as he wiped down the already immaculate countertop. "Most people use that World Wide Weird thing instead these days."

"Well, you know, that luck might be better if you'd let me leave a stack of these," Xander coaxed. He fanned the remaining handbills.

Tate shook his head. His soda shop was an old one, and he was quite experienced at saying no to teenagers. "You clear the space, you post, one post per event. No handouts. Them's the rules."

"Right you are, Mr. Tate!" Xander said. He didn't press the issue; he didn't want the owner to change his mind. Instead he thanked the proprietor again and exited, the door's bell ringing as he reemerged into the late afternoon sun.

It was time to start strategizing, he realized. So far

he'd just been going door to door, but it was late enough in the day that at least some local operations would close their doors soon. It made sense to select the most likely options, in terms of both friendly management and likely clientele. Six doors down was a familiar storefront that promised both.

"Of course!" Xander said softly. "That's the ticket."

A moment later another door swung shut behind him, and another old-fashioned bell chimed. He took a deep breath, drawing in not the sweet goodness of ice cream and syrup, but something richer. Herbs and spices and incense filled the air.

"Welcome to the Magic Box," came a girl's voice. She didn't sound very enthusiastic. "Let me know if I can help you find something, but we close in, um, twelve minutes."

Perched halfway up a ladder was the latest in a long run of Magic Box clerks, taking inventory of items on an upper shelf. She was dressed in black slacks and a tank top, and had purple hair. In one hand she held a clipboard, and in the other, some kind of wizened root thing that looked like it had seen better days.

"I just wanted to see if I could post a notice," Xander said. The sight of purple hair stirred a memory. This had to be the girl Cordelia had mentioned, the girl who'd witnessed weird doings at the Bronze.

The girl sighed and set the items she held aside. She didn't so much descend the ladder as jump from it. Her booted feet thumped on the Magic Box's floor. "Gimme," she said, and took the proffered handbill. She stood near him as she read.

Close-up she was cute. She was older than Xander, but not by more than ten years. Under the pale makeup and dark lipstick, her features were elfin, and he could tell that she kept herself in shape. This had to be Aura's on-the-scene informant. Just below one shoulder a badge announced her name.

"You're Amanda?" he half-said, half-asked. He was interested now. As he'd told Cordelia earlier, he was a healthy teenage boy.

Still reading, the clerk grunted in acknowledgment. Unlike almost anyone else he'd spoken to, she seemed determined to read each word on the orange sheet. After what seemed like an eternity she wrinkled her nose and looked up from the page. "I dunno," she said.

The Goth girl had pretty eyes, he realized. They were hazel and they sparkled, even in the shop's subdued lighting. Xander was really interested now. She had a certain eerie charm, but without any evidence of the supernatural strings that usually came attached to girls with wrong-colored hair.

"You don't know whether you're Amanda?" he joked.

"Yeah, I'm Amanda, and yeah, I'm new," she said. She was less preoccupied than he'd thought. She tapped the orange sheet. "I don't know about this," she said.

"The Magic Box has always been a good friend of Sunnydale High and the local business community," Xander said hopefully. "Band candy, yearbook ads, concert announcements, the whole schmear." He pointed at the window, where sun-faded remnants of older postings lingered.

Amanda was reading the drive-in announcement again. He wondered if she wanted to memorize it.

"Look," Xander said, ingratiatingly. It was time to turn on the famous Harris charm. "This is a good spot. We're running a horror movie, and with the creepy-crawlies who come in here sometimes—"

Her head came up, as if on a string. Her hazel eyes flashed. He'd said the wrong thing.

"Sometimes," Xander repeated. "I said, 'sometimes.' Some of my best friends shop here. Honest." He paused, trying to make up for lost ground. "Look, I can throw in a couple of passes, if you'd like."

He showed her the tickets. She plucked them from his fingers and read both sides carefully. Finally, grudgingly, Amanda nodded. "Okay, deal," she said. "And if the boss complains, it comes down."

"Fair enough," Xander said. "More than fair, really."

It took a few minutes to scrape an old posting of the same appropriate size from the window's glass, but less time to tape his new one in place. While he worked, she set the door's lock and flipped the door's sign to SORRY, WE'RE CLOSED. She did it with remarkable speed and had already begun to count the day's receipts by the time he'd finished.

"You're done?" she asked, sorting bills. The hint wasn't very subtle. It was time for Sign-Posting Lad to vanish into the sunset.

"Yeah," Xander said. He watched her count for a moment. "Busy day?" he asked.

"I thought you were done," Amanda said. Coins clinked as she sorted them into the appropriate compartments. Clearly, she wasn't one for small talk.

"Can I ask you a question before I go?" Xander said slowly. He tried to choose his words carefully, but that kind of premeditation didn't come easily to him, especially not with girls.

"That's one already," she said. More coins clinked.

"Have you ever been to the Bronze?" There was a chance she could tell him more about what had happened the previous night.

The sound of coins being counted came to an abrupt halt. The purple-haired girl looked up from her work, dark lips parted in an amused grin. Xander knew instantly that he hadn't spoken carefully enough.

"You're wasting your time, townie," she said. "I don't date kids."

At the time of its original grand opening decades before, the drive-in had stood at the town's outermost fringes. Sunnydale had grown since then, but in other directions. Specifically, toward the new state highway and the connector roads to the federal interstate, so the open-air theater still lay outside its border. The distance and relative isolation helped save it from vandals and scavengers. Once the original management had reclaimed its projection and sound systems and stripped the concession stand bare, there simply hadn't been much left behind to attract visitors.

Angel had been one of the few visitors. His restless nature had led him to explore Sunnydale in some detail since coming there, and he knew the town better than most natives did. Now, in the dead of night, he stood on the hill overlooking the previously abandoned establishment and marveled at how much it had changed in such a short time.

Even at a distance he could tell it was ready to reopen. The parking area was weeded, reterraced, and strewn with fresh gravel. The speaker posts were gone, presumably superseded by broadcast sound. The screen's refurbished surface gleamed faintly under the autumn moon. A shiny new marquee was positioned near the box office.

"Very nice," Angel said to no one in particular. Like himself, the place was a reminder of a time gone by, even if its time was not as far past as his own. As an institution the drive-in had enjoyed its heyday in the 1950s, and some years of that tumultuous decade had been very good for Angel. Seeing the drive-in brought a smile to his pale face and made him think of Elvis and early rock and roll. As with most of Angel's smiles, however, it was faint and faded quickly.

With long, easy strides he made his way down the hill and to the theater's perimeter. Renovation extended to a hastily erected cyclone fence topped by razor wire, but neither posed any obstacle worth noting. A single leap carried Angel over the barrier, and he set about exploring in earnest.

Yet again the vampire's keen senses proved useful. He could see perfectly in the moonlit gloom. His touch and hearing were sensitive enough that he had no difficulty picking construction site padlocks or inspecting the newly installed projectors. As far as he could tell, there was nothing particularly sinister about the place.

Certainly, there was no trace, however faint, of any kind of werewolf. Even the paperwork he found in the construction shack was in perfect order. Whoever Shadow Amusements, Inc. was, they managed their contractors well.

The phantom memory that Angel had dredged up earlier still pointed this way, but the thought was really an absurd one. The fact that it hadn't paid off didn't really surprise him.

The last structure he looked at was secure, relatively speaking. It was the concession stand building, which also housed the operation's office behind a heavy door with a good lock. Angel needed nearly a minute to pick the locks on both doors, and then he let himself into the sparsely furnished space.

He started with a shelf anchored to the wall above the desk. It held a dozen thick catalogs with elaborate logos on each spine. The light inside the office was too faint for color, but judging from the images that Angel viewed in monochrome, the covers were impressively gaudy. He moved closer to the office's single window, hoping for enough moonlight to discern any more details.

They were booking catalogs used to arrange movie rentals. Angel flipped through one, uninterested and unimpressed. He was reaching for a second catalog when he heard the sound.

Outside, freshly strewn gravel crunched beneath one footstep, then another. Someone was approaching. Hastily he rammed the catalog back into place and cursed himself silently. He'd left the building's door ajar.

"I know someone's in there," said the person, presumably a guard. One of the files in the construction shack included a contract with a local security service. Angel said nothing.

"Let's do this the nice way," the man outside said. "I've already called the police, and I warn you, I'm armed."

Angel heard the *click-click* of a double action revolver's hammer. That was bad. Bullets couldn't hurt him, but they stung like the dickens, and there was always the danger of ricochet. He didn't particularly want the guard to get hurt just for doing his job.

The vampire considered his options. One was the half-open door, with the armed guard on its far side. The other was the single window. It was old, and heavy beads of rust had welded the metal frame shut. The glass was thick and reinforced with embedded wires. He could break through easily enough.

Angel heard the door behind him start to swing open. He gripped the window's sash firmly. Metal shrieked as the corrosion of decades tore free. The opening was barely big enough to admit him, but he squeezed through, grimacing as his jacket caught a jagged edge and tore.

His feet had hardly cleared the window frame when the guard fired. Thunder roared and the night was lit brightly for a split second. Rock dust flew as a bullet buried itself in the parking lot's gravel.

A moment later the guard's head extended cautiously from the open window. He looked from side to side, then drew back. When he spoke again, it was in clear, businesslike tones. Angel could hear him perfectly from his hiding place.

"Ralph, this is Murray again," the guard said. Angel couldn't see inside the office, but it was easy to guess that the other man had a cell phone. "Yeah, Murray at the site. It's not an emergency. Looks like there was a break-in, but the perp is long gone." He paused. "Okay, I won't call them 'perps' anymore." He paused again, then lied. "No, I didn't fire my gun," he said. "I know better than that."

Finally Murray spoke again. He sounded both apologetic and exasperated. "Yeah, Ralph, yeah. I *know* false alarms are a pain. I'll come by tomorrow to help with the paperwork. Right, first thing."

There came a click as he closed his phone, breaking the connection. The guard poked his head out the window again and looked from side to side a second time.

"Huh," he said softly, speaking to himself. "No footprints at all. This place must be haunted."

Angel, watching him from the rooftop above, thought otherwise.

Chapter Five

Buffy sat slumped beneath the chestnut tree on the school campus. The day was very young, with only the earliest of early-bird students reporting for duty, but Buffy's eyes were already heavy-lidded and bloodshot. She leaned back against the tree's trunk, the open history book in her lap nearly forgotten. Next to her on the dew-damp grass was an unopened pint of orange juice and three chewy granola bars. She was too tired to eat.

"Good heavens, Buffy," Giles said with concern in his voice as he approached her. "You look dreadful."

"No wonder you're a bachelor," she said. Even her voice was colored with fatigue. "With patter like that, I mean."

"That's not what I meant," the master librarian said. Dropping his briefcase, he squatted beside her. She could tell he that he didn't want to get grass stains on his tweed trousers. "Were you out all night?" he asked, plainly concerned.

She nodded. "Pretty much," she said, closing her history book. "Went home, did the dinner thing with Mom, pretended to go to bed. Slipped out later to go on patrol."

Giles nodded. It was a story he'd heard before.

"One thing led to another," Buffy continued. "By the time I realized the night was gone, the night was, well, gone. Went home, changed, and raided the fridge." She forced a smile. "And here I am, bright-eyed and bushy-tailed."

Giles picked up the orange juice carton and opened it. "Here," he said, "drink."

"In a moment," she said. "I want to tell you—"

"Drink," Giles said again. "Your stamina is remarkable and so is your dedication. Neither will suffer if you tend to your blood sugar."

Buffy drank. The OJ was still cool, and it admittedly felt good coursing down her throat. Almost immediately the world became a brighter place. "Um," she said. "Good."

Giles nodded. "Now," he said, "tell me what happened."

"That's just it, Giles," Buffy said. "Nothing happened."

He looked at her blankly. "Nothing?"

"Nothing at all," she said. "The night was dead. Not even a teensy-tiny vampire to be seen. I lugged twenty pounds of pointy weapons for nothing."

"You tarried on patrol all night because nothing happened?" Giles asked. Concern began to give way to annoyance. "Buffy, as I said, I admire your sense of duty, but—"

"You weren't out there, Giles," Buffy said. She looked in the direction of the parking lot. The first real wave of students began arriving. Xander might be among their number, she realized, and she safely tucked the granola bars into her pocket. "It felt like the whole world was holding its breath."

The words came to her without conscious thought, but they rang with absolute truth, even in her own ears. Once more the night air had been filled with an electric charge, but this time there had been no incident. For nearly seven hours she had patrolled the haunts and byways of Sunnydale, her nerves humming and her entire body tensed for action that never came. She was exhausted now, more tired than mere lack of sleep could have made her. Buffy felt like a sprinter who'd spent the entire meet on the starting line, without ever having a chance to run.

Giles stood, and offered his hand. She waved him aside and rose in a single fluid motion, as if her body were a wave that had decided to flow uphill. It was Buffy's nerves that felt the worst of the night's fatigue, not her body.

"And Angel?" Giles asked. "Did he make an appearance?"

She shook her head. Her relationship with the vampire was one of trust and even love, but it was not without its mysteries. "No show," Buffy said. She tried not to sound wistful. "Business of his own, I guess. Happens sometimes."

They walked together toward the school entrance. Sitting had been a mistake; moving made her feel better. So did the companionship. The orange juice had probably helped too. She began to feel hungry and patted the granola bars in her pocket.

"You were supposed to contact me last night," Giles said in mild reproof. "Before patrol, I mean."

"Ouchie," she said. "I'm sorry. I forgot." She didn't tell him that she had visited Willow and researched the drive-in. Bad enough that she'd slighted him; it would make things worse to tell him that the effort she had undertaken instead had been fruitless. "Any luck in the home library?"

He gave a brief nod. "Possibly," he said. "Do you know what an *excursus* is, Buffy?"

"Something that used to be a curse?" she asked.

They were inside the school now, and the hallway was slowly filling with students. None seemed to give the mismatched pair a second glance. Even now, Buffy wasn't exactly Miss Popular, and his official role as school librarian often made Giles the next best thing to an invisible man.

He tut-tutted softly. "No, no," he said. "It's not an occult term but an academic one. It's a lengthy discussion of a specific topic, appended to another, larger work. Often they're published separately, after the 'parent' book."

"A super-footnote," Buffy said. "A footnote from the doomed planet Krypton."

He gave no sign of having heard her. "I keep certain excursuses at home, even when the parent volume resides in the collection here. They're very rare, very fragile, and—"

"And you don't want me spilling any orange juice on them," Buffy said. She paused in midstride. They were at the library entrance, which meant it was time for her to report to homeroom. Classes could be cut, if the procedure were executed right, but missing homeroom meant being marked absent, and she'd missed too many days already.

"Just so," Giles said. "I think they may be useful in the matter of the mis-shelved book."

"The missing book, you mean," Buffy said. She still had her doubts about that Inga character.

"The missing book," Giles said patiently. He made the three words sound like a great concession. "We should speak of it at length."

"I now call this meeting of the Secret Justice Club to order," Xander said. He stood at the head of the long table, hands at his hips, and drew himself up to his full height as he eyed the three seated girls. It was a very dramatic pose, and a good match for his portentous tone. "Thank you for convening here, in our secret citadel of justice, on such short notice."

Seated beside Willow, Buffy looked at him with hooded eyes. She was far more durable and resilient than even an Olympic athlete, but even so, fatigue from the long, stressful night left her irritable. Her friend's clowning wasn't helping things either. "Xander—," she started to say.

He gestured with one hand, waving her input

aside. "No, no, Slayer Lass," he said, with mock-condescension. "I realize we all have hectic schedules, and I appreciate you all making time in your lives—"

"Put a sock in it, Xander," Cordelia said, speaking even more sharply than Buffy. She drummed perfectly manicured nails on the table's polished top. Whichever social event the gathering had taken her from, she wanted to get back to it, even more than Buffy wanted to rest.

Xander flinched at the words. He looked at her, as he had at Buffy, but he didn't wave her words aside. He seemed confused and paralyzed by indecision, like a deer in headlights.

"Yes, Xander, put a sock in it," Giles said, suddenly behind him. Hearing the American colloquialism in his arch British tones made Willow giggle softly.

Xander shut up, taking the empty seat next to Cordelia. He shrugged and remained silent, but looked upward as if to say, "Why me?"

Ordinarily well groomed, Giles looked a bit rumpled now. He'd pushed up his sleeves and opened his collar. A lock of brown hair dangled onto his forehead, glued by perspiration. Without preamble he began, "I stayed here late last evening, conducting a total inventory of the occult holdings." He gently set three dusty volumes on the table. "It's a painstaking task and demands some concentration, as I'm sure you all understand."

"I'm sure we do," Willow said softly. Buffy elbowed her, but the Rosenberg girl still smiled. Of the five gathered in the school library, she was the only one who seemed genuinely relaxed and happy.

Giles continued. "What I found was disturbing," he said. He glanced at Buffy. "You were right," he said. "The book that I thought might have been mis-shelved is missing."

The Slayer smiled broadly, pleased with herself.

"That's not good news, Buffy," Giles said.

Buffy's smile faded.

"The book is nowhere on the premises," Giles said. "I inspected the stacks as well."

"So Inga took it," Xander prodded. "So you complain to Snyder, or we go to the nurse's station—"

Buffy shook her head. "No," she said, after Giles had nodded permission to interrupt. "I checked on that yesterday. We don't have a Nurse Inga."

"Well," Willow said. "She didn't last long."

"That's not what Buffy means," Giles said. "I confirmed it with the administration. Not only is Mrs. Forman still the school's attending nurse, she's very happy in her role. No one else has interviewed for her job, or even applied for it."

"Oh," Xander said. He blinked, as the meaning of the words sank in. "Oh!"

Giles nodded. "It appears we've had an impostor," he said. "I can only assume that she was sent on some manner of reconnaissance mission. Now—"

"Not an impostor," Xander said, interrupting.

Cordelia nodded in instant agreement. "Impostors," she said, emphasizing the plural.

At Giles's prompting, and in short, precise sentences, she told the assembled group about Xander's and her near-encounter in the courtyard. Being Cordelia, she emphasized points that the others didn't find nearly as interesting as she did: the disappearing cheerleader's outdated hairstyle and unfamiliar school colors. "Even after that, we checked some more," she continued. "She wasn't in any of the classrooms, or anywhere else she could have gotten to. I even checked the girls' locker room."

"I offered to," Xander pointed out.

This time it was Xander who got an elbow in the ribs, and not from Buffy. He winced and eyed the ceiling again.

"And you were going to tell us about this when?" Buffy asked.

"Now," Cordelia said in simple explanation.

"Well, in the future, in events of an occult nature—," Giles began.

"It was a cheerleader," Cordelia said, raising her voice. "Not a werewolf or a vampire or a hobgoblin. I had drills and homework, and, you know, it's not like I get to use any of my study periods to actually *study* anymore!"

No one had anything to say to the outburst. For a long moment the library was nearly silent, the only sound was the *tap-tap* of Cordelia's fingertips, which she had begun drumming again.

"Yes, well," Giles said at last. He seated himself and reached for the first of his books. As he fanned the pages, dust billowed from between them and hung in the still air.

"A girl's got to have her priorities," Cordelia said.

"And it's not like I can't hold my own against any girl from another squad."

"We agreed to tell you about it together," Xander said, sounding conciliatory. He smiled very slightly as Cordelia shot him a grateful glance. "And, like the lady said, we're talking cheerleader here, not creepy emissary from the outer darkness."

"There's where you may be in error," Giles said mildly, still paging through his book. He tone was mild, but he quickly moved into lecture mode. "Tell me, do any of you know what ectoplasm is?" he asked.

None of them answered. He shook his head sadly before continuing. "Ectopolasm is—"

"The visible but immaterial substance that makes up the physical composition of ghosts and similar occult manifestations," Buffy said, cutting him off. She spoke with the singsong cadence of someone reciting from memory. She smirked.

"Very good," Giles said, impressed.

"There's another definition too," Buffy said. "For biologists. Outer part of a cell."

"That won't be necessary," Giles said, clearly a bit chagrined. "You've proved your point. You're up to date on your readings. Good show."

"So we're working with ghosts?" Willow asked. "Like, maybe Sunnydale High is built on an old nurse's cemetery, or Cordy's phantom cheerleader was from the class of '52?"

"Believe me," Cordelia said, "those have *never* been the school colors." She spoke with great disdain. "I don't care *how* far back you go."

"Tell us about the books," Willow said eagerly. She liked books. "The ghosts and the books."

"I don't know that they're haunts," Giles said. He seated himself and steepled his fingers, considering how best to explain. "You must understand, many of the books that I've brought with me are from the Council archives, very old and difficult to replace. Even the least of them date back to a time when books were hand-bound and produced in very small number for highly demanding patrons."

"Yeah, yeah, yeah," Buffy said. "Written in human blood, bound in human skin—"

"No," Giles said forcefully. "Or, rather, not entirely. I refer more to much younger books, typeset rather than hand-scribed. The nature of the production process was such that it discouraged specialization. Books tended to be compendia, rather than focused works."

"Okay," Buffy said, she nodded. "Omnibi."

"Omnibuses," Willow corrected. The eyes of both Cordelia and Xander began to glaze, but neither said anything. Perhaps they didn't want to prolong the discussion.

"I won't trouble you with the titles," Giles said. "But someone seems to have absconded with four key works addressing the mechanics of what we now call psychic phenomena." He paused. "These were what passed for scientific works in their day. Sections deal with mindreading, mesmerism, transubstantiation of souls and base matter, spiritualism, psycho-etherics, even phrenology." He glanced at Xander. "That's the study of head bumps," he said.

"I knew that," Xander said, but he didn't look like he expected anyone to believe him.

Giles resumed. "One thing that all four books have in common is that they have sections pertaining to ectoplasmic constructs."

"Ghosts," Buffy said.

"Or something similar," her watcher agreed.

"The ghost of a werewolf?" Buffy asked skeptically.

"Not necessarily. It could be something more complex," Giles said. "And, at any rate, we cannot be certain that those sections are why the texts were taken. The commonality among the books *is* intriguing, though."

"You really know your stuff, Giles," Willow said, awestruck.

"Yeah, I mean, I can't even keep my comics straight," Xander said, only to receive a withering glance in return.

"I know the collection well, but I don't have them memorized," Giles said. "I do maintain an annotated catalog, though. That's how I was able to identify the missing works and get at least an approximate idea of their contents." He paused. "They aren't particularly noteworthy volumes. Many books of greater rarity and importance were on the same shelves."

"But what does any of this have to do with the wolf-man?" Buffy asked.

"Possibly nothing. But it may have everything to do with him, and with Nurse Inga, and with Cordelia's cheerleader."

"Hey, she's not mine," Cordelia said.

No one acknowledged the comment. After a long moment of silence Buffy bit the bullet and fed Giles the prompt. "Well?" she asked.

"I think our measure's being taken," Giles said. Even under his habitual reserve, his voice carried a concerned quality. Something that was not quite worry colored his words as he continued. "I think that, whoever our visitors are—whatever they are—they're here to investigate us, and the extent of our knowledge." He looked at Buffy pointedly. "Perhaps of our strength, as well."

"So we're talking minions here, huh?" Xander asked.

Giles nodded.

"But—but why use something so, well, goofy?" Willow asked.

"Whatever do you mean?"

Willow fidgeted a bit. She traced an idle pattern on the tabletop as she chose her words. "I'm just saying it's funny," she said. "The details are all wrong. The wrong school colors, the wrong kind of werewolf. If they aren't haunts, why not get the details right?"

"I don't know," Giles said. "But as I explained to Buffy earlier, I have some additional materials at home that may provide some clarification. Until then, I urge you all to proceed with the utmost caution."

Jonathan was well aware of his place in the overall scheme of things. Fit but short, shy, timid, and studious-looking, he was not so much an also-ran in the Sunnydale High rat race as he was a spectator on the sidelines. The faculty and other students didn't particularly dislike him; they scarcely realized that he shared their world. He was as close to a nonentity as you could get. That accounted for his wary expression when Xander sat in the chair across from him at the cafeteria table.

"Hey, J," Xander said. He deployed his meal, arranging plates, bowls, and a drinking glass in front of himself before setting the plastic tray aside. "Anyone sitting here?"

"Um, no," Jonathan said. No one ever sat across from him.

"Mind if I join?" Xander had gotten three desserts and was arranging them in order of preference—banana pudding, chocolate cake, gelatin mold.

Jonathan watched without comment. Harris sure could eat. His own meal came from home and was much more modest: egg salad on rye toast, and barbecue-flavor potato chips.

"I don't mind," he finally said. Even to his own ears, his voice sounded nasal and reedy. He surprised himself by asking the obvious question. "Where's Buffy?"

"Huh?" Xander asked, pausing with a forkload of mystery meat halfway to his mouth.

"You usually hang with Buffy Summers," Jonathan said. Life on the fringes gave him a good vantage point for observation. "Her and Rosenberg. You guys are always together, and it's like you live in the library or something."

Jonathan refrained from mentioning Cordelia, even though he'd noticed Xander and her engaged in quiet conversation several times recently. Xander was higher on the social ladder than Jonathan was, but only by a few rungs. Cordelia Chase was at the top. The idea that Xander and Cordelia might spend time together was difficult to process.

"*Ocupado, mi amigo,*" Xander said, mangling each word. He ate what appeared to be Salisbury steak. That was one thing he had in common with Buffy Summers: a healthy appetite. Maybe when they were in the library they researched recipes and swapped cooking tips.

"*Ocupado?*" Jonathan asked.

"Spanish for 'occupied,'" Xander said, with an air of imparting great wisdom. "That leaves you and me more time for manly-man talk, my friend."

Now Jonathan felt a twinge of worry. He had a passing acquaintance with Xander—less passing than with some other students, perhaps, but still only a passing acquaintance. They had their chance encounters on campus and ran into each other at the comic shop and the video club, but that was pretty much the extent of their interaction. Why had Xander joined him for lunch? More important, why was he calling him "my friend"?

Xander finished his entrée of overcooked steak patty with bad gravy, limp green beans, and runny mashed potatoes. He indicated Jonathan's food. "You going to eat those chips?" he asked.

"Of course I am," Jonathan said, and ate one to

prove his point. It tasted good, so he ate another, then nibbled his sandwich again. He wondered if Xander would take the hint and go away. Xander clearly didn't want to eat alone, but Jonathan was used to it and didn't mind.

"Yep, manly-man talk," Xander said. He drank half his carton of milk with a single gulp. "The companionship of men. There's nothing like it, is there, my friend?"

"Buffy and Willow were too busy for lunch, huh?" Jonathan asked, trying to keep Xander on-topic. He didn't ask how many others had been busy too. He knew that, socially speaking, the little Levenson boy was the court of last resort.

Xander nodded, reluctantly. He said, "Dumb ol' girls." His generally clownish expression gave way to a halfhearted scowl. "I am just about tapped out on the ladies just now."

Jonathan sighed. It was time to take the bull by the horns. "What are you up to these days, Xander?" he asked, careful not to make the question a challenge. "What can I do for you?"

"Ask not what you can do for me," Xander said. "Ask, rather, what I can do for you."

Xander rummaged in a pocket and drew out a handbill. He slid it across the table. He'd been distributing the sheets in the hallways and courtyard, even on line in the cafeteria. Jonathan eyed the sheet warily. Clearly, Xander had forgotten that he'd already given him one.

Jonathan wasn't surprised.

"You *do* know what a drive-in is, right?" Xander asked. When Jonathan nodded, he continued. "Ever been to one?" he asked. "Want to?"

The elevator chime sounded; the cage had reached the penthouse level. Jim Thompson looked at his reflection in the gleaming metal doors one last time, verifying that his tie was straight and his hair neat. Word was that the gent in the penthouse was a heavy tipper, and Jim didn't want to give him any excuse not to live up to his reputation.

Everything looked fine. The wheeled cart's burden of covered dishes, utensils, and glasses rattled and clinked as he pushed it along the carpeted hallway. When he reached the appropriate door, he rapped on it once.

"Room service," Jim said.

"Enter," came the response. The voice was cultivated but strong enough to be heard clearly, even through the door. "It's not locked."

Jim obeyed. Wheeling the cart into the room, he got his first glimpse of the penthouse's occupant, who was seated at the small desk that matched the rest of the suite's furniture.

He looked pretty much how the hotel's day manager had described him. He was lean and well dressed, wearing a dark shirt and linen trousers that reflected the easily elegant style of the very rich. He sat ramrod straight, with perfect posture. Four books lay on the desk before him. They looked old and were big, at least as thick as telephone books, and he closed the one he'd

been reading as Jim entered. Even that simple movement, the occupant made with a certain panache. Jim
was impressed.

The only detail the day manager had gotten wrong
was the color of the guest's hair. Jim had been told that
it was white, but it was gray, not the gray of an old man
but the gray of iron. Jim wondered fleetingly if he'd
dyed it, then dismissed the thought. Who would color
his hair gray?

"Your lunch order, Mr. Belasimo," Jim said.

"Balsamo," the man corrected him, standing.

Jim winced. "Sorry, sir," he said.

"That's quite all right," Balsamo said. His eyes
twinkled. "It's not a common name in this part of the
world, or in this day and age." He looked at the cart,
waiting.

One by one Jim removed the covers and indicated
individual courses. "She-crab soup," he said. "Caesar
salad. Roast beef, center-cut, with asparagus and fresh
bread. Mixed fruit."

"Capital," Balsamo said. He'd already lifted the
wine bottle and was examining the label. He nodded in
approval and returned it to its caddy. "You can put all
of this on the dining table," he said. "Open the wine but
leave the covers. I'm not quite ready to eat lunch yet."

Jim nodded. With quick, practiced motions, he
arrayed the meal and utensils. As he opened the bottle,
he asked, "Will there be anything else, sir?"

"Possibly," Balsamo said, eyeing him. "What's
your name, young man?"

"Jim Thompson."

"Tell me, Jim, are you a native of Sunnydale?" he asked as he opened a wallet that was as limp as wet silk. He pulled a bill from it.

"Yes, sir," Jim said. "Born and bred."

"I understand that Sunnydale is a town were things happen," Balsamo said.

Jim knew what he meant. His own life (so far) had been straightforward and without incident, but you couldn't live in Sunnydale without hearing stuff. Jim heard a lot, much of which he preferred not to believe, but there was no way that at least some of the stories weren't true.

"Well, yes. Yes, sir, it is," Jim said.

"Put the meal on my bill," Balsamo said. He passed Jim a bill. "This is for you."

Jim sneaked a peek. His eyes widened. It was a fifty. "Thank you, sir!" he said.

"Not at all," Balsamo said warmly. "But tell me, Jim, what time does your shift end?"

"Um, three o'clock," Jim said. "Are you interested in a tour or something? The concierge prefers that guests make arrangements through his office." What the concierge really preferred was that the hotel staff not make extra money on the side.

"No, not at all," Balsamo said. "But I would like to speak with you some about your fair city and about the things that happen here; a native perspective would be especially useful." He smiled. "I'm quite prepared to compensate you for your time."

Chapter Six

"Fine! Go! But if you get in trouble, it's on your mother's head!" Mr. Harris shouted as Xander ducked out the door, car keys grasped in one hand. "I'm warning you!" his father continued. "You only get one call at the police station, and it better not be to me!"

The door slammed shut behind him, muffling his dad's angry tirade but not blocking it out completely. Even worse, his mother joined in, and the two adults' voices rose in angry confrontation. Once outside, the specific words were hard to pick out, but words really didn't matter. The overall tone was plain: The Battling Harrises were at it again. Embarrassed and ashamed, Xander quickly made his way to the family car, hoping desperately that no one in the neighborhood would pick that minute to look outside and see him.

If he could still hear the rising argument, so could the neighbors. Xander wasn't in the mood for sympathetic glances.

The car started easily enough. Xander turned on the radio and listened to soft rock as he drove into the gathering dusk. He had plenty of time.

The drive-in's management had billed tonight's grand opening as a special sunset to sunrise show, but working on-site had taught him the truth behind the advertising lie. Sure, the projectors would come to life as soon as the sky got dark enough to serve as an outdoor theater, but the big screen would present nothing of note for an hour or so.

Xander stole a look in the rearview mirror. Already his family home had disappeared in the distance. If only all his troubles could be left behind so easily.

The Levensons lived fairly close, and he found their home without incident. Jonathan was already waiting for him at the curb. Xander pulled over and gestured for his classmate to get in.

"Hey," Jonathan said. He looked some fractional degree more at ease than Xander had ever seen him before. He was dressed more casually, too, in jeans and a jersey, with a light Windbreaker in case the night got cool. He carried a medium-size paper bag, spotted with oil, which he set between them as he buckled up.

"Sack?" Xander asked.

"Popcorn," Jonathan said.

"Sweet!" Xander said, surprised by the considerate gesture. He kept one hand on the wheel but used the other to scoop unearthed fluffy white kernels into his mouth. He chewed and swallowed, then continued. "Salty, I mean."

"Maybe we should stop somewhere and get sodas," Jonathan said.

"Nah, drinks are on the house," Xander said. He reached into the backseat and hoisted a small cooler, then set it down again. "Just like admission."

Some minutes and miles passed as they drove to the theater before Jonathan broke the silence.

"Y'know," he said. "At first I was surprised when you invited me to this."

"Mmmm?" Xander said. His mouth was full again.

"Uh-huh," Jonathan replied. He hadn't taken any of the popcorn but was staring raptly out the window. It was as if he thought the world's secret lay somewhere in the night beyond. "No one invites me anywhere, Xander. I figured the girls all turned you down."

"That's not true," Xander said, but he felt a pang of something like guilt, nonetheless.

"S'okay," the shorter boy said. "And, the way I see it, there's one good thing about going to the movies with another guy."

"Oh?" Xander asked, suddenly vaguely nervous.

"Uh-huh. It's better than going by yourself."

A dozen thoughts flitted through Xander's mind, images and sound bites summoned up from the depths of his memory. He thought of Cordelia's admonition against taking another girl to the movies, and he thought of how breezily Buffy had declined his over-tures so many times during the preceding months. He remembered the smirk of dismissal he'd gotten from the Goth girl with the pretty eyes, and how readily he'd accepted it. For some reason he even recalled the plaintive way that Willow looked at him sometimes, when she thought he couldn't see her.

"It's a melancholy truth you speak, my friend," he finally said. The words made him feel worldly wise. "A melancholy truth, indeed."

TDQYDJP's gig was only through Thursday. Taking the stage tonight was another band, much worse and much louder. Their music sounded very much like the wailing of damned souls, and Cordelia could only understand every third word.

"What the heck is 'German Dungeon Rock'?" Harmony asked. Her barbed words cut through the fog of background noise that filled the Bronze between sets.

She wasn't looking for any real answer to her question, Cordelia knew. Queries like that were one of the many ways Harmony had of complaining.

"I don't know," Cordelia told her for what felt like the hundredth time. She wasn't enjoying herself. Harmony was well into petulant mode, and that was never fun. Most nights the other girl made an appropriately supportive audience, but not tonight. Part of the problem was that Aura hadn't shown, and Harmony was usually at her best in a group setting. Experienced one on one, as a central attraction rather than as part of an ensemble, she grated.

"I mean, it doesn't have a good beat," the blonde continued, as if she hadn't heard Cordelia. Maybe she hadn't; the background chatter was pretty loud, and the Bronze's DJ had picked some particularly obnoxious tunes for between-sets play.

No plain vanilla rock tonight, Cordelia realized as sounds like a cat being killed blared from the sound system.

Harmony was on a roll. "I mean, I don't think you can dance to this stuff," she said. She leaned forward and sipped from her glass's bent straw, then scowled. "Empty," she said, sounding like a very little girl having a very bad day. "This whole evening is a bust."

Cordelia continued to pay her as little attention as possible. Instead, trying not to be too obvious about it, she alternated between scoping out tonight's crowd and sneaking peeks at the Bronze's entrance. Tonight's crop of club-goers was sparse; worse, most either repelled or bored her. Too many were known quantities, fixtures on the Sunnydale social scene, and the rest were unsavory types drawn by the evening's attraction.

That could change, though. Cordelia hoped it would. There was always a chance that someone new and interesting would arrive. She'd even be happy to see Buffy and the gang, provided that Xander played things cool. That wasn't going to happen, though, since Buffy was likely on patrol and Xander was sure to be at his stupid drive-in.

She wondered if he was having fun. She hoped so, as long as it wasn't *too much* fun.

"I just wish Aura would show," Harmony prattled on. "She hasn't been in school for two days now." Her eyes brightened. "Hey!" she asked eagerly. "D'you think she, you know, ran off with that wild one from the other night?"

"Without telling us about it?" Cordelia asked tartly. "Don't be silly. Maybe she's sick."

There was a line at the ticket booth. Xander craned his head and tried to count the number of cars and trucks between the Harrismobile and the theater entrance. He gave up at twenty, partly because his neck got tired and partly because the line was moving with relative speed.

"You need money?" Jonathan asked.

He hadn't spoken much since being picked up, and Xander knew why. They really didn't have a whole lot to talk about. The realization was a humbling one, but nothing new.

"Nope, I told you," Xander said. "We're guests. The boss-man insisted."

The car moved forward in fits and starts as the patrons ahead of them paused to pay. That changed when they finally reached the box office and the ticket seller waved them through with a nod of recognition. Xander snuck a side glance to see if Jonathan was appropriately impressed, then guided the Harrismobile forward, negotiating the gravel bed of the parking lot easily. He was on familiar territory now.

The drive-in's basic shape was a bowl—a shallow one, lopsided and irregular. At the time of its birth, more than fifty years before, construction crews took advantage of a natural depression in the hills surrounding Sunnydale. With bulldozers and steam shovels they had deepened and customized it, terracing some two thirds of its curve to provide raked parking. Dead center in the remaining curve was the brick and steel-girder shell of the great screen, support for the lightweight, reflective curtain. Those two steps had constituted the major portion of the effort; the concession stand, projection shack, and other appurtenances had been minor in comparison. Everything that original crew had done, they'd done well.

Xander told Jonathan the story as he guided the car toward the reserved parking for staff and guests. "They built to last in those days," he said. Hanging around on the construction site earlier in the week had given him new appreciation for construction work and the men who did it. "The place closed down in the 1980s, but it has held together since then."

"Why'd it close?" Jonathan asked as they passed another rank of parked cars. Dusk was giving way to night, and it was hard to see into the other vehicles, but he seemed determined to give it a try.

"Don't know for sure," Xander said. Just in time he saw an opening in the line of cars and took advantage. Someone, somewhere, tooted a horn in greeting as he did. He chose to believe that the greeting was for him and made a vague wave in return. "Home video and rising gas prices conspired to—"

"That's not what I mean," Jonathan said, interrupting. That wasn't something he did very often. "I looked it up on the Internet. You know what state still has the most drive-ins in operation?" he asked.

"Um," Xander said, "I'd hazard a guess, but I think you're about to tell me."

"California," Jonathan said, with a nod.

Xander nodded. That made sense. California still had a fair amount of relatively open countryside, and Californians were remarkably tenacious in their love of driving.

"So why not here?" Jonathan asked, pressing the issue.

"Don't know," Xander said again.

He pulled the family car into an available slot, set the brake, and killed the engine. Before them stood the great curved screen that he'd watched a team of contractors reinforce and resurface. Just now its gleaming white exterior presented the image of a local car dealership.

"Sound?" Jonathan asked.

"Oh, right," Xander said. He turned the dashboard radio on and set it to the appropriate frequency. The car's interior filled with the voice of his favorite local DJ, extolling the virtues of a particular make of auto.

He grinned. The show was about to begin. This was going to be good.

The kettle whistled and Giles extinguished the stove burner, making the merry sound fade. He poured healthy measures of the boiling water into his teapot and teacup and returned the kettle to the stove top. Silently he counted to ten. Satisfied that the pot had warmed properly, he drained it, then put the loaded filter basket in place. He poured water again, through the tea leaves, and smiled as steam scented the small, tidy kitchen of his home with the rich, almost medicinal aroma of his preferred blend. Almost as an after-thought he emptied the china cup, also properly warmed now, and placed it on the service tray beside the pot. The entire ritual was oddly comforting, a reminder of his home, so far away.

He took the tray to his desk. As the tea continued to steep, he made a quick check of the effort's current status.

He'd only just begun, really. Three books lay open on the desktop with specific passages indicated by careful application of those insipid little yellow slips that the Americans had come up with. The books were secondary works, rare and desirable by some criteria but pedestrian by Watcher standards. The books' authors were not true adepts but disciples, dilettantes, and dabblers, with the good fortune to study more ele-vated tomes, if not to own them. They'd studied such works as the *Crimson Chronicles* and the *Pnakotic Manuscripts*, and then attempted to record the knowl-edge and processes in words of their own. A surpris-ingly high percentage had perished horribly under suspicious circumstances, but their derivative books had uses. They weren't essential to the work Giles did, but sometimes they served as what Willow Rosenberg might have termed "backups."

The excursuses were a different kettle of fish entirely. They were derivative too but were the prod-ucts of superior minds, specialists in specific aspects of the occult. The four excursuses stacked at his left elbow were fragile and rare, so Giles stored them in Mylar sleeves that Xander Harris had obtained for him at a local comic-book shop.

Giles slid the first from its transparent envelope. Hand calligraphy, the letters and words elaborately intertwined, nearly filled every page. The document was made of some kind of thin leathery substance, and Giles knew from personal experience that it could not be photocopied. Any attempt to do so, with any machine, merely resulted in blank, wasted paper.

His tea was ready. Giles poured a cup, added a bit of sugar, and sipped. Perfect. He would have preferred a bit of brandy, but the night's work demanded his full attention and a clear mind.

Two of the excursuses were specific to the missing books. One was a treatise on ectoplasm; the other, a discussion of transmigration, the transfer of living souls between vessels. *The Book of Dorahm-Gorath* addressed many more topics, of course, but he had to work with what he had on hand. The idea was to cross-reference the excursuses with the secondary works and arrive at an approximation of the source document. He'd not be able to reconstruct all of the contents, but he had to start somewhere. It was a process akin to triangulation.

Giles read and made precise notes on the sheets of a yellow legal pad. He sipped his tea as he worked. The clock ticked as the hours slid by and the remaining tea turned cold.

He had just correlated an excursus reference with a passage in his well-worn copy of *Secrets of Alchemie and How to Profit Thereby* when someone knocked on his door.

"Odd," he said softly, after a glance at the clock. The hour was late and he hadn't been anticipating company. Perhaps it was Buffy dropping by while out on patrol?

Distracted, he started to gather books and work sheets into an orderly stack. Giles trusted himself to sip tea in an orderly manner, but he remembered all too well how casual the Slayer had been with her lunch shake.

Knuckles rapped on the door again.

"A moment, just a moment!" Giles called. Slightly irritated, he opened the door. "I do hope you realize the hour. It . . ."

His words trailed off as he saw his visitor. He blinked and laughed, a chuckle that sounded nervous even in his own ears. "Oh, my word. It can't possibly be Halloween yet," he said.

And then he said nothing else at all.

Chapter Seven

Sunnydale's warehouse district was quiet after sunset. Streetlights were few and far between, and the worn, weathered buildings loomed darkly against the night sky. Even the pale glow of the moon served only to accentuate the shadows.

Buffy liked to come here at least once a week, to look for signs of trouble or habitation. The nooks and crannies of the big old commercial buildings made good hiding places for vampire nests. Other times they served as way stations for the various occult artifacts that kept making their way into the city, and way stations for the people who traded in those artifacts.

She moved with easy grace though the night, not calling attention to herself but not trying to hide, either. Her feet gritted audibly on the cracked and dirty pavement, and she didn't shirk the yellowish radiance of the one-per-block streetlights. One of many reasons that she'd made such a success of herself as a Slayer was that she looked like a victim: young and slight, with girlish features and bouncing blond hair. In an imagined vampire restaurant, "Today's Special" would have looked very much like her. Buffy's only real concession to the night's work was her weapons cache, hanging by cross-strap from one shoulder, like a paperboy's bag.

After the incident with the wolf-man, she wanted to keep her hands free.

Without trying to be too obvious about it, she eyed the surrounding darkness. Darkened doorways and darker alleys made good hunting stations for vampires, and right now, a plain ol' garden variety vamp would have been a relief. Though she'd never admit it, the past two nights had unnerved her, just a teensy-tiny bit. First there was the ambush by the surreal wolf-man, who fell so far outside of even Giles's knowledge and expertise. Then there was the persistent electric tension, the never-relieved sense that something terrible was going to happen. After two restless nights the easily recognized menace of fangs and bloodlust would be almost welcome. Sometimes familiar was good.

She managed a smile at the thought. Who would have believed that something like killing vampires could ever become routine? But that was precisely what had happened over the course of long months since she'd accepted, however reluctantly, the life of the Slayer.

For now, nothing seemed amiss. No vampires, no wolf-men, no demons—no nothing, really, except for the electric buzz of aging streetlights and that odd burnt smell that old buildings get. Even the sense of lurking menace that had gnawed at her for two nights now abated slightly.

Either that or she'd gotten used to it. Sooner or later, anything that persisted long enough became routine. Her own life had taught her that.

She paused for a moment, bathed in a streetlight's pale glow, and mulled the possibility. It seemed unlikely, but still . . .

That was when she heard the roar of engines approaching.

On the huge screen's curved expanse was the gigantic image of a half-dozen men on chromed motorcycles, huge against a field of black asphalt and blue sky. They were big men, burly and strong, clad in ripped blue jeans and leather jackets or vests. Most let their hair and beards fly wildly in the wind, and only a few wore any kind of headgear at all. Those few looked very wrong; rather than safety equipment with tinted visors, they wore German-style army helmets with broad, low rims. One had a spike on top. Guitar music blared, strident and emphatic.

"I thought the cheerleader thing came first," Jonathan said, but he didn't take his eyes from the screen. The image was bright enough that hints of color flickered across his face.

"Cheerleader last," Xander said. He spoke as if explaining the natural order of the universe to a novice. "Kung fu first."

"The marquee says—"

"Kung fu first," Xander said again. "Take the word of one who knows. Anyhow, this is just a coming attraction."

As if in response, a deep and booming voice thundered from the parked car's sound system, louder even than the guitars. *They were the dark knights of the road and their horses were the two-wheeled, road-ripping, fuel-injected, rampaging machines they called 'hogs'! The highway was their hunting ground, and decent people were their prey!*

Management had programmed the grand opening not just as a festival of vintage films but as a recreation of the "authentic drive-in experience." Before and between movies there'd be coming attractions for action flicks of the past, chosen to appeal to modern audiences. Xander had spent an entire afternoon in the projection shack as it underwent renovation, chatting up the man who was running the films now. He'd taken a peek at the projection schedule, and thus had known for days what he could expect to see tonight.

The reality was different, though, and the difference was increasingly apparent as Xander munched and sipped his way through the preview for *Hellions on the Highway*. Images that seemed small and remote at home, even on the largest monitor, had new impact when blown up to fill the drive-in's screen. They became so much larger than life, in more ways than one. Not only did they loom above their audience, but they took on a luminous quality as well. Xander had witnessed some remarkable things in his life, but when the preview zoomed so close that the lead biker's glaring eyes nearly filled the screen, even he was impressed.

"Yow," he said softly, then ate more popcorn.

"They're the kings of the road, and you'd better pray their *road doesn't lead to* your *town!"* the announcer warned.

The din started faintly in the distance, barely even a murmur at first. But the murmur became a rumble and the rumble became a roar, and then the roar gave way to a rolling thunder. It sounded like a thousand bombs being detonated all at once, and then, impossibly, detonated again and again and again. The thunder grew louder, becoming more intense.

It was the roar of motorcycle engines, and they were coming closer.

Buffy turned just in time to see the first headlight glare at her from the night's darkness. Almost instantly the single beacon was joined by five more like it, moving together in a formation that spanned the street and sidewalks alike. Looking past them, she could barely see chrome shining in the shadows beyond. The headlights' size and placement, the grumbling roar of high-power engines, and the hints of glinting chrome all added up to one thing.

A motorcycle gang was bearing down on her, moving hard and fast. She didn't waste time wondering who or how or why.

With urgency but not fear Buffy looked from side to side, assessing the immediate terrain's strategic possibilities. A fire-escape ladder offered a potential avenue of retreat, but she'd need to turn her back on her pursuers. A narrow alley promised escape too, but it was thick with unexplored shadow. A loading dock to her left offered shelter and high ground and a wall for her back. It also offered the potential for being cornered, but right now it seemed like her best bet. She sprinted toward it.

The Slayer moved fast, but the leftmost motorcycle moved faster. With an engine snarl like the cry of a great cat, it raced into Buffy's path, obstructing her from her goal. The rider was a show-off, pulling his bike back and up into a wheelie as it rushed past her. Buffy caught a glimpse of torn jeans and a leather vest covering bare, hairy arms, thick with muscle. She saw a low-brimmed helmet and glaring eyes, and a lashing, whirling something that shone like silver even in the poor lighting.

It was a chain.

Buffy ducked back, nearly in time but not quite. The leading link of the lashing chain smashed into her shoulder. It hurt like a bullet, and she gave a gasp of pain.

The first biker roared past her, his job done. He'd delayed her just long enough for his fellow bikers to join him. With practiced ease, the five followers formed a circle with Buffy at its center. Even as she realized what they were doing, the first bike retraced its path and joined them. The now six bikes roared in a chrome-steel orbit, a whirling wall that blocked off any possible path of escape.

They'd surrounded her.

Buffy let her legs bend slightly and dropped into a half crouch, presenting a smaller target. She groped in her weapons bag and drew out her crossbow, with bolt already in place. Without looking, she cocked the weapon and set its release, then reached again into the store of weapons. Working by touch alone, she found her battle-axe. It was the only other instrument that might be suitable for distance work. With an axe in her left hand and a crossbow in her right, she looked warily from side to side, poised for battle. When the attack came, it would come quickly.

"Yee-haw!"

"Whoop-whoop-whoop!"

"Little lady want a ride?"

The shouts and mocking calls were loud enough to be heard over the bike engines, at least when they were this close. The six gaps between the six bikes narrowed, and the circle became smaller. In perfect coordination, they were closing in on her, like a sprung trap, or a closing noose.

When had this become her life?

At the barest edge of her vision, Buffy saw a liquid silver flash, the sheen of chrome steel rippling like water under the streetlight's glare. Another chain. With animal instinct she jumped straight up. Pavement chips flew as the chain struck where her feet had been. At the peak of her trajectory, in the perfect instant before gravity pulled her earthward again, Buffy took easy aim and squeezed the crossbow's release. The bolt flew.

One of Buffy's tormentors yelped in pain as the

arrow stabbed him. Buffy's feet and the injured rider's bike struck pavement simultaneously. Sparks flew as the motorcycle, engine still roaring, spun on its side across the pavement.

"First blood!" one of her attackers yelled.

"Yeeeee-haaawwww!"

"Time to party!"

"Gonna getcha! Gonna getcha good!"

The circle of death grew tighter. Her crossbow was empty now, its bolt flown. She cast it aside. Even as she did, a third chain lashed at her, then a fourth. Buffy dodged them both, with an awkward twisting leap. If she fell, or if she drifted too far from the center of their circle, she'd be in serious trouble.

Yet another whiplash arc of steel whistled at her. But this attack arrived at chest height, offering an opening.

The axe's handle was a shaft of cured and seasoned wood that was a bit longer than her forearm, banded with reinforcing steel. She gripped it with both hands just beneath the axe's bladed head. She was running on automatic, executing moves that Giles had drilled into her during long hours of combat practice.

The axe came up, not to strike but to block. Buffy's two-handed grip tightened as she held it before her, precisely perpendicular to the whipping chain's trajectory and as far from her body as she could manage. Instinctively, she braced herself for impact.

It came like a thunderbolt. It raced through her arms and body, almost enough to tear the weapon from her hands.

Almost, but not quite.

She'd timed it just right. Night air whistled as the chain wound itself tightly around the axe handle, like fishing line on a reel. Buffy gritted her teeth and dropped back, yanking hard. The chain came with it, and the biker roared curses as she tore the lash from his grip and made it her own.

Buffy now held one end of the chain, spinning it rapidly above her head. She grinned. Numbers were still on her attackers' side, but her reach was as long as theirs now, and her strength was far greater.

"Somebody wanted to party?" Buffy shouted.

She braced herself and cast the chain in a sweeping, serpentine strike. As much by luck as by aim, it hit a biker and wrapped itself around one beefy arm. The man yelped in pain and lost control of his bike. More sparks flew as the second bike toppled and slid across the pavement, taking the biker with it.

Most of him, at least. Either Buffy's whiplash strike had been stronger than she realized, or her assailant's structure was physically weaker. His arm remained trapped in the chain's coils, torn free from his body. The grisly image lingered just long enough to register before the arm vanished into nothingness.

If she'd had any doubts that these guys were like the man-wolf of a few nights before, those doubts were gone now. The kid gloves could come off; they weren't human, probably not even alive.

"Okay!" Buffy shouted defiantly. "No more Ms. Nice Slayer!"

The remainder of the pack pulled back. She

grinned, pleased with herself. She had them on the run. She spun the chain again.

That was when it happened. One second the captured chain was secure in her grip, reassuringly solid as its centrifugal force tried to pull it away from her. The next second, without warning, the seemingly solid metal evaporated to liquid, and then was gone.

Turning to her empty hand, she blinked. The bikers were like the wolf-man, but so were their weapons. *Could things get any worse?*

As if on cue, a figure dropped from the night sky.

A woman's voice, deep and throaty, purred from the car speakers. She had an accent that promised vague exoticism without suggesting a specific nation or language. Whoever she was, wherever she was from, she seemed very pleased to have found an audience.

"The Swedes have a word for it," she said. *"But doesn't everyone?"*

Jonathan's eyes widened a bit, and he sat more upright in his seat. He set his drink in its arm-rest caddy and pulled his other hand from the bag of popcorn, without taking any. His entire attention was fixed on the drive-in screen, where a very attractive blonde was winking at him and everyone else in the audience. She had cleanly drawn features and pursed lips that were as red as a fire engine. Her eyes were of the purest blue, and if her hairstyle and makeup were a bit old-fashioned, there was no doubt that they got the job done.

"Hel-lo," Xander said softly. He set his drink down too.

"Um?" Jonathan asked. Words seemed to come from somewhere deep inside him, slowly and with great reluctance. "Are we old enough to see this?" he asked.

"Why, yes, spoilsport, we are," Xander said dreamily.

"Are—are you sure?" Jonathan spoke with a mixture of relief and uncertainty.

"It's just the coming attraction," Xander told him. "The movie, now—"

The blond woman on the screen moved seductively as she made her way down a long hallway with many doors. She wore a white uniform and wheeled a cart loaded down with medical equipment. When a pudgy, balding man dressed in white approached from the opposite direction, she tickled his chin and kissed him on one cheek before whispering something in his ear. He blushed furiously, and Xander knew that no matter what language the blond woman spoke, he wanted very much to hear it.

Movie content had been the topic of more than one discussion during the previous week or so. Historically, drive-in films were known for their racy content and approach, but "racy" had meant different things over the years. According to Xander's supervisor, the new proprietor's fondness for the old-fashioned extended to a certain conservativeness in programming. This preview was as much of the movie as they were ever likely to see, at least at this venue.

"From a land of cold nights and hot passion comes a prescription for health and happiness," the announcer cooed. *"Really, it's* The Best Medicine."

As she spoke, the movie's title appeared on the screen in bold pink letters, then faded. Replacing them was another close-up of the pretty blond nurse, her lips pursed in an alluring smile.

As the screen faded to black, the announcer's voice sounded again. *"Report for treatment to this theater,"* she said. *"Ask for Nurse Inga."*

Xander sat bolt upright, not an easy thing to do in a car seat. "Inga?" he said sharply.

"Inga," Jonathan agreed. "That's what she said. Why?"

Xander didn't answer. Telling Jonathan about the phantom nurse on the Sunnydale High campus would have meant telling him entirely too much. Anyway, the matching names had to be a coincidence.

Didn't they?

Night air whistled in Angel's ears as he leaped from the warehouse rooftop.

As he fell, he changed. His perpetually youthful features shifted into something bestial and cruel. His brow dropped and his jaw thrust forward. His eyes receded into their sockets slightly and burned with animal fire, while picture-perfect teeth became ragged fangs. By the time he smacked into his target motor-cyclist, he was in full-on vampire mode.

"Angel!" Buffy said.

He didn't answer. Instead, even as the big high-horsepower bike bucked and slewed, he wrenched the German-style helmet from the biker's head and threw it away.

"Hey! Wha—?" the biker yelled. "What's your problem, man?"

Hands that were inhumanly strong clamped on to either side of the rider's head. Angel gripped and wrenched. The biker roared in pain. He took both hands from the handlebars and tried to break the vampire's grip, but without success. The motorcycle broke ranks and went into a skid.

Angel expected to hear bones break, but instead he felt something tear. The biker gave a final yelp and then fell silent as his head came up and away from his shoulders, slightly more easily than he would have expected. Angel had only the briefest moment to consider the surprising development before the disconnected cranium evaporated, leaving nothing but empty space between his hands.

Then the rest of the biker melted away.

As did his motorcycle.

Angel found himself several feet above the ground, trying to ride a motorcycle that was no longer there. He dropped, bounced, and rolled. Returning to his feet, he threw himself back into the fray.

In some ways, the world moved in slow motion for a vampire. Angel's inhuman speed and fast reflexes made it easy to dart between two of the four motorcycles that remained, still circling his beloved. In seconds he was where he belonged, at Buffy's side.

"That was a surprise," the Slayer said. She'd reverted to a defensive stance, battle-axe in one hand and curved *boka* in the other.

"Pleasant one, I hope," he said.

"More the merrier," she responded.

She offered the machete-like blade to him, and he accepted it gratefully. The weapon's hilt felt good in his hand, reassuringly solid. Right now the sensation of substantiality was precisely what Angel wanted.

The four remaining bikes continued to circle. They too looked substantial—solid masses of muscle, bone, and metal. It was difficult to believe that mere physical force could turn them so swiftly from something that *was* into something that *wasn't*.

Angel's travels had exposed him to many religions and philosophies. A lesson from one drifted up from his subconscious. It was a Zen koan, a puzzle or question that was intended to teach and enlighten.

Where does a fist go when the hand opens?

Wherever it was, the vanished biker had gone there too. Angel had seen many things in his long years, but this specific phenomenon was something new.

He could worry about that later, though. It was time to finish the job.

Guitar chords blasted, fast, fat, and fuzzy. They echoed as the camera tracked down from the orange sun that filled the screen, sliding down along a yellow sky to seemingly endless sands that were the color of pale rust. Just watching it all made Xander feel hot and sweaty. It didn't make sense to start the car and run the air conditioner, so he retrieved a second soda out of the ice-filled cooler instead. It was the cheap stuff, supermarket-brand carbonated fruit punch, but it went down good.

On-screen, the desert sands seemed to stretch on forever. Where they met the yellow sky, something was increasingly visible. It was a man riding a horse.

"This is going to be good," Xander said. When he got no response, he glanced at Jonathan. The younger boy's eyelids were half-closed. "Hey!" Xander said sharply.

Jonathan sat up, startled. "Huh? What?"

"It's kind of early to doze off," Xander said. He would never admit it, but he had prepared for the evening by taking a nap after school.

"No, no," Jonathan said. "Just resting my eyes."

Xander had his doubts, but he allowed another abrupt guitar riff to command his attention back to the screen. Just in time, too; a jump cut eliminated the distance, and a man's face nearly filled the screen. Presumably, this was the distant rider shown a moment before.

He looked as though he'd been built out of beef jerky, as though the desert sun had sucked every molecule of moisture out of his body and turned his skin to leather, corrugated and rough. He had a Stetson hat pulled low over eyes that were little more than slits but that still burned with a fire all their own. A hand as leathery as the face raised a cheroot cigar to barely parted lips. The traveler took a puff and exhaled, and the swirls of smoke condensed into yet another movie title.

Reach for the Sky—and Die!

"They hardly make westerns anymore," Xander said helpfully. He drank more fruit soda. If he kept this up, he realized, he'd need to try out another part of the renovated open-air theater.

"Gee, I wonder why," Jonathan said. He'd opened a cooling beverage as well, but his choice was caffeinated cola.

"This one's Italian," Xander said, still trying to be helpful.

The guitar chords continued. The rider's face gave way to a rapid-fire sequence of images, some of them surprisingly violent. Having dismounted his horse, the man strode along the central street of a flyspeck western town. Storefronts, saloons, and plank sidewalks lined either side. He carried a sawed-off shotgun in one hand and a six-shooter in the other, and a bullwhip coiled around one serape-clad shoulder. In a series of tightly edited shots, he put all three weapons to extensive use.

The shotgun blasted twice, taking out the saloon's plate glass window. When townsfolk made their opposition known, booming shots from the six-gun silenced them . . . permanently. The bullwhip snaked out to impossible length, snared a rooftop sniper, and pulled him to the street. Interspersed between the frenetic scenes were glimpses of quieter moments, ones in which the characters exchange challenges, quips, and double entendres. When he spoke, the leathery-looking man's voice was as dry and raspy as stones sliding across one another. And because the film was dubbed from the original Italian, his lips never quite matched his words.

Reach for the Sky—and Die! the screen read

again, and Xander grinned. Less than an hour into the festival, and he felt he'd already gotten an admission price's worth of entertainment—and he hadn't even had to pay.

Buffy and the others didn't know what they were missing.

Six against one had become four against two, now that Angel had joined the fray and stood at Buffy's back. The odds weren't great, she thought, but they were improving. Aside from inexplicably vanishing when their heads were torn off, their attackers hadn't manifested any other paranormal attributes to speak of. The biker-gang members seemed to be pretty close to baseline human—rambunctious and antisocial human, but human all the same, at least in terms of strength and durability.

Not to mention smarts, she realized as one of the bikes broke formation. Its rider had forfeited the advantage to try to strike at her with a length of chain doubled up like a club. The move was a mistake on the rider's part, and Buffy was more than willing to show him why.

"Watch this," Buffy said over her shoulder. There were moments when she liked showing off; besides, it was her turn. Angel had taken the last one.

The rider's spiraling track brought him close, then closer still. The chain lashed out as the biker swung his weapon in her direction. Buffy swung too, slashing the battle-axe in a short, perfectly timed arc. The steel head's razor-sharp edge intersected with the biker's arm just above the bend of his elbow. It passed through the arm as easily as it would have through flesh and bone. Forearm and chain spun away into the night.

The biker screamed a bad word. With his remaining hand, he twisted his handlebars hard and gunned the bike directly at her. The bike reared up. The rider screamed something at her, barely audible over the engine's roar but clearly very, very impolite. His eyes gleamed in the streetlight's yellow glow, and the chrome of his motorized steed flashed. Every muscle in Buffy's body tensed. Her mind was moving so quickly that the world around her seemed to have shifted into low gear.

She had to time things perfectly. Drop again into the barest beginnings of a crouch. Grip the battle-axe and get ready to swing. When the biker's close enough—too close to change course—spring to one side and chop at him again. The moves were simple stuff, things she'd practiced with Giles countless times, but the moment had to be just right.

The moment never came. As the motorcycle's front wheel raised and the big bike poised like a snake to strike, it began to fade. Adrenaline still pushed her senses into high-speed overdrive and slowed the world around her. For the first time Buffy saw what happened next not as an event but as a process. The outlines of both bike and biker wavered and softened. Their colors faded and what had been solid and real became misty and translucent, like a fading photographic image.

"Buffy, look out!" Angel shouted, from what seemed like a world away.

The bike's front wheel came down. He was trying to pin her between knobby tire and dirty pavement. She still had time to dodge, but she already knew that the need to do so was gone.

The biker's mouth was open, but no sound came out. He was fog now, and then less than fog. Looking up, she found that she could look *through* him, and see the waxing moon beyond. Then he was gone completely.

"Wow," she said softly. "Wicked cool!"

The remaining bikers peeled off and beat a hasty retreat. As the last went, Angel hurled the blade she'd given him, aiming squarely at the last rider's leather-jacketed back. By the time it should have struck, the target had vanished.

"In the back?" she asked Angel, one eyebrow raised, as her world shifted back into normal gear. This wasn't the first time she'd experienced the time-dilation effect.

Her vampire paramour shrugged. The battle had come to an end, and as if to commemorate that fact, his features reverted to human-normal. As they softened and shifted, he said, "Seemed like a good idea at the time. I knew he wasn't human."

"I'm wondering if he was even alive," Buffy said.

"Ghost?"

It was Buffy's turn to shrug. "Dunno," she said. "Giles has a bug up his nose about spook stuff, though." With a few quick sentences she summarized the library briefing. By the time she finished, her breath and pulse were normal again.

They spent the next several minutes looking for evidence, but there was none. The only signs that the bikers had ever been there were secondary: tracks in the street's oil and dirt, and scrapes where the first, toppled bike had slid along the asphalt. There was no tire rubber, no metal trace or paint transfer, not even the scent of exhaust fumes. Once again it was as if their attackers had never existed.

"Busy night," Angel observed. He'd gone to retrieve the *boka* and was loping back to her now.

"Yeah," Buffy said. She almost smiled as she remembered her own complaints about the previous night, the long hours of wary tension and waiting for action. Someday, she thought, she'd need to count her blessings. "It was either that or go to the movies," she said.

"Movies?" Angel asked.

"Xander's thing," she reminded him.

He nodded as he fell into step with her, clearly intending to accompany her on the rest of her patrol. "I went out there," he said. "Did some looking around. If that place is a festering hellhole of occult evil, I can't see it."

But to Buffy's practiced ears he sounded like he had his doubts.

Chapter Eight

"*I'll always be a cheerleader in my heart*," said the girl on the movie screen. She had long dark hair that fell to her shoulders like a waterfall. She pulled the handsome premed student closer to her for a kiss that was long and slow. When at last they came up for air, she continued, "*Always. But I'll never be lonely again!*"

The credits began to roll. Xander blinked and rubbed his eyes. He was only half-awake. Eight hours of movie watching was a *lot,* and it seemed to him that the quadruple feature had stretched on even longer than the dashboard clock said.

Four features, uncounted coming attractions, a cartoon, and miscellaneous concession stand spots had filled their night at the drive-in. Xander had spent longer periods watching television at home, of course, but that was at home, sprawled on a well-worn couch with a remote control within easy reach. The marathon drive-in experience was something altogether different, even with the preparatory nap.

Xander's eyelids drooped and his muscles were sore. An insect or two had bitten him. Half a sack of popcorn and nearly a gallon of supermarket soda pop had left his mouth feeling mighty funky. He rubbed his eyes some more, then stretched and yawned, making each breath a deep one. Gradually full consciousness returned. With a tight grin he turned the key and started the engine

"Wow, what a great night!" he said softly.

He meant it too. Xander had enjoyed every minute, and even with the morning-after consequences, he logged the night solidly in the plus column. The film festival had been a nightlong peek into a world he'd missed by being born too late. The broadly drawn characters, the cartoonlike action, and the goofy plots struck a nerve with him. The drive-in was like a comic book come to life, just not a very good one. Asian men executing flying kicks, elderly aristocrats with chainsaws that roared, inmates rising up to free themselves—all of those were very neat things, indeed.

Sometimes the not-very-good comics were the best ones.

The car engine coughed once or twice, then came to life. Through the windshield the drive-in screen read GOOD NIGHT, FOLKS. DRIVE CAREFULLY! And beyond the screen, the dark bowl of the night sky displayed the barest streaks of pink. The morning sun approached. It was time to go home.

"What did you think, Jonathan?" he asked.

The only answer was a soft snore from the seat beside him. Levenson had conked out sometime during the closing credits for *Mysteries of Chainsaw Mansion,* the second movie. Xander had prodded him awake, only to lose him again during *Caged Blondes.* The poor little guy didn't get to see a single minute of *The Lonely Cheerleader.*

"So much for companionship," he said, backing the car out of its parking slot. He was one of the late-stayers; at least three quarters of the massed cars had left an hour or more before. Even so, the Harrismobile wasn't the last car to roll slowly along the gravel-lined exit route. To his amusement, at least a dozen parked cars remained, their interiors dark and their occupants vague in the pre-morning gloom.

"Some people don't know when they've had enough of a good thing," Xander muttered, accelerating slightly. Gravel sprayed up from the roadbed and rattled against the car's undercarriage. "Hear that?" he asked, in a louder voice. "That's the sound of horse-power, my friend!"

Jonathan snored some more.

Xander took his eyes from the road long enough to glance at his passenger. Jonathan was out like a light. He was slumped against the car door with head lolled back and mouth hanging open.

That wouldn't do, Xander decided. He reached across the space between them and poked the other boy's shoulder, gently at first and then with more vigor. "Wake up, little Susie," he said.

No response.

"JONATHAN! WAKE UP!" Xander said again. This time he'd shouted loud enough in the closed confines to make even his own ears hurt.

"Grnk?" Jonathan said, startled. "Huh? Wha—?" He looked around himself, first at Xander and then at the pre-dawn world as it rolled by outside. "We're going?" he asked.

"Uh-huh," Xander said. Some idiot had come to the event in an extralong SUV, and half the oversize vehicle extended from the parking slot, blocking Xander's path. He edged around it and tooted his horn in irritation. There was no response that he could see or hear.

What the heck were these people thinking? The show was over and it was time to go home.

"Cheerleader?" Jonathan asked.

"Very lonely," Xander said. "A masterpiece of the motion-picture art form."

It was only half-true. Xander's own flirtation with drowsiness had come sometime during the fourth and final film—naturally, the one he'd wanted to see most, if only so that he could needle Cordelia about it. Even so, something about the flick had gnawed at him. Half-awake, half-asleep, he'd had a moment of insight about the events of the film. Now an insight about the movie bubbled somewhere just below the threshold of his conscious mind. It was like the answer to a question on a history pop quiz, the stray bit of knowledge that you knew wouldn't be available for use until long after you wanted it. The more he tried to dredge the thought up, the more it evaded him.

"Oh," Jonathan said. He sighed, but the sigh morphed into another snore.

He was still snoring when Xander pulled up in front of the Levenson house. This time Xander couldn't wake him. The best he could do was coax Jonathan halfway to awareness. With Xander guiding him, the kid moved like a sleepwalker as he opened his front door and tottered inside.

"Thanks for coming, J," Xander said.

"Grphl" was all he heard Jonathan say before the door slammed shut.

"Xander! Oh, my heavens, Xander!" Hands grabbed his shoulders and shook him. "Xander, wake up! Please wake up!"

"Huh? Wha—?" Xander said, his voice fuzzy from sleep. He struggled a bit, but something wrapped itself around him. Adrenaline rushed through him. Was he under some kind of attack?

"Wake up, please!" It was a woman's voice. It was probably a woman's hand that slapped his right cheek, barely enough to sting but hard enough to make a loud popping noise.

"He's probably drunk!" A man's voice, more distance but louder, boomed in his ears. "Out all night! I warned him!"

Xander's eyes opened. His hand came up, just in time to intercept a second slap. He blinked at the worried-looking woman leaning over his bed.

"Mom?" he said. He disentangled himself from the sheets and scooted back in his bed, partly to sit and partly in case another slap was coming. Slapping was a wake-up trick that played better in the movies than it did in real life.

"Oh, thank heavens," Mrs. Harris said. "I was so frightened!"

"Mom, what's wrong?" he asked.

"You were asleep and you wouldn't wake up—"

He was bleary-eyed but could see enough to read his clock radio's display. It was only nine a.m., he realized with a shock. "Mom," he said. "We talked about this! I was out all night! Of *course* I was sleeping late!"

"I know, I know," she said. "But I was so worried."

"Tell the boy I warned him!" his father boomed from somewhere down the hall. "He's lucky I don't come in there and tell him how lucky he is!"

His mother was near tears, and even his dad seemed pretty worked up about something. Suddenly, he had a bad feeling about the situation. "Mom, I'm fine," he said. "What's wrong? What's happened?"

"It's Jonathan Levenson," she said.

"Jonathan?" Xander asked. The bad feeling became a *really* bad feeling. "I dropped him off on the way home."

"I know," Mrs. Harris said. "His parents called. They found him on the living room floor."

Saturday breakfast was eggs. Joyce had whipped up what she called a "sort of omelet," incorporating bits of ham and cheese with bits of leftover veggies from previous meals. As so often happened with such improvised dishes, the whole was more than the sum of its parts.

"This is delish," Buffy said, raising another forkful. She and her mother were seated in the breakfast nook, and the morning sun's rays streamed in through one of the large windows.

"Thank you, dear," Joyce said. The praise pleased, but it frustrated, too; she knew that she'd never be able to recreate the dish exactly.

"No, really," Buffy said, and favored her mother with a glance. "You've been watching PBS again, haven't you?" she asked in mock-accusation. "All those cooking shows, with those French gigolos!"

Joyce shook her head. She ate some of her own serving and realized what Buffy meant. There was something vaguely exotic about the mélange of egg and oddment. For such a humble meal, it tasted surprisingly sophisticated. "Just some spices," she said, at a loss for any more detailed explanation.

Several textbooks sat in a tidy stack next to Buffy's elbow. Their presence at dinner would have been unacceptable, but in the morning, on a weekend day, they were welcome indicators of rare studiousness on Buffy's part. Joyce knew her daughter was a bright girl, and gifted in so many ways, but Buffy really hadn't seemed to have found her path in life just yet.

"What are your plans for today, dear?" Joyce asked.

"Study," Buffy said.

That certainly sounded like a fine idea to Joyce. "That's good," she said, offering up a bit of positive reinforcement before moving on to more challenging ground.

Buffy nodded. Her plate was almost clean, but one last slice of toast remained on the serving dish between them. She made a questioning glance in Joyce's direction and, after noting a nod of permission, took the piece of bread.

"Xander, Willow, and I are getting together," she said. "Maybe Cordelia."

The enthusiasm in Buffy's voice dropped a bit with the last words, but Joyce chose not to notice. When Buffy had first begun classes at Sunnydale High, she'd never wanted to talk much about her schoolmates. Cordelia Chase had been one of the exceptions, and the subject of regular grousing on Buffy's part. That seemed to be changing. Joyce didn't know how and she didn't know why, but to judge from some of Buffy's recent comments, there seemed to be the barest chance that the two girls were becoming friends, at least of a sort. As far as Joyce could tell, that pretty much had to be for the good; the Chases seemed to be a good family, and her daughter could always use a friend.

"You and Cordelia seem to be getting along well lately," Joyce said lightly.

"Things change," Buffy said, not quite as lightly. "But think of it as an armed truce. Or that détente thing."

"You're growing up," Joyce said hopefully.

"That's one way to look at things," Buffy said. Her expressive eyes took on a faraway look and she smiled, very faintly, as if at a joke that only she knew. A joke, or a kind of truth.

Buffy was hiding something, Joyce knew. Her own

teenage years weren't so long gone that she couldn't remember the way things worked. Secrets were part and parcel of life, never more so than in the adolescent years. Whatever the secret, she could only hope that it wasn't too serious.

She soldiered on. "Maybe you could have Cordelia over for dinner sometime . . . ," Joyce started to say.

"Oh, yeah, like *that's* going to happen," Buffy replied with an air of absolute dismissal.

It was time to change the subject. Joyce took a breath, trying not to be obvious about it. "You were out late last night, weren't you?" Joyce asked. She made the question a gentle one.

Bite, chew, swallow, speak, then bite again: Buffy had it down to a precise system. Unfortunately for Joyce, her question had come at the beginning of the sequence, so she had to wait for an answer. That gave her daughter a chance to think things through before responding, Joyce knew, but there was nothing to be done for it.

Buffy swallowed. For good measure she lifted her glass and swallowed again, orange juice this time. At last she said, "Yeah, later than I'd planned. It wasn't a school night, and—"

"It's all right, Buffy," Joyce said. "I noticed, that's all." She liked to think that she noticed more than her daughter realized.

"Uh-huh," Buffy said.

"With Xander and the others?"

"Xander was at the movies," Buffy said. She finished her toast and drained the orange juice.

It was a non-answer, but Joyce decided to let it pass. "What are you going to study, then?" she asked.

"What aren't I going to study?" Buffy asked, ungrammatically. She ticked items off on her fingertips one at a time. "History," she said. "Biology. Philosophy. And I promised Willow that I'd pretend to understand what she talks about."

"So you'll be at the Rosenbergs?"

"Probably," Buffy said. She nodded but looked away, and Joyce knew that she was lying. No, not lying; more likely, she was shading the truth. That was part of being a teenager too, and the signs were obvious to a parent, if one knew how to look, and Joyce did. "For a while, at least. I'm supposed to drop by Giles's, too. He promised to loan me some research materials, from his personal collection."

"You're spending a lot of time with him, too," Joyce said. The function that the school librarian held in her daughter's life still loomed as a bit of a mystery. Well educated, soft spoken, and quite refined, he seemed every inch the proper gentleman. He was old enough to be Buffy's father. Despite that, he seemed to have settled into a role that was as much friend as mentor.

"Giles is okay," Buffy said. Coming from her, that was high praise for any adult. "For a stuffy ol' Brit, I mean."

"That's not nice," Joyce said. "He's doing you a favor."

"I meant it in a nice way," Buffy said mildly. There was no more food to be had, so she dropped her used utensils onto her empty plate and began to clear the table. "And, believe me, Giles just loves doing stuff like this. He's got books coming out of his ears, and he loves to show them off." She paused. "That sounds grosser than I meant."

"Call him before you go, then," Joyce said.

Buffy's response came in phases. First there was the clatter of plates and flatware being stowed in the dishwasher, followed by the *glug-glug-glug* of detergent being poured. Then, as the much-appreciated appliance hummed to life, Buffy picked up the kitchen phone and dialed.

Without meaning to pry, Joyce watched the transaction. She watched as Buffy looked first patient, then irritated, and, finally, worried. The expressions flowed one into another, like a plant blooming in time-lapse photography.

"That's funny," Buffy said, returning the receiver to its cradle. She didn't sound like she thought it was funny at all, though. "There's no answer."

Gravel rattled against glass, a familiar sound. Willow set aside her computer mouse and went to the window. This really wasn't the time of day for such subterfuge. There was no reason why any visitor simply couldn't come to the front door and ring the doorbell like civilized folk. She opened the window and said as much.

"I'm sorry," Xander called up to her from the lawn. His words were apologetic but his tone was slightly irritable, and it was easy to see why. He looked very tired, with shadows under his eyes. "Old habits die hard."

They'd known each other most of their lives. That wasn't a terribly long span of time in absolute terms, but from Willow's viewpoint it was forever. She could remember sneak-watching Christmas specials on television with Xander, an interest that her parents didn't entirely approve of or even understand. She had a bit of a crush—more than a bit, really—on Xander, and had watched with increasing anxiety as he threw himself at one girl after another, never taking time out for her. Buffy was among the most recent targets of his unrequited affection, which had lent an interesting texture to their friendship of late.

"You could have called," she said, mildly chiding. Xander was a welcome guest at the Rosenberg home, but a girl liked to have a little warning.

"No, Will," Xander said sourly. He was sweating a bit in the late-morning sun, and Willow thought it made him look sexy. "No, I couldn't."

"Why not?" she asked.

"Because I'd need a phone to do that, and that means I'd need to surgically remove it from my mom's ear," Xander said testily. His handsome features formed a half scowl. "The MNN is in on the air."

"M-N-N?" She pronounced each of the letters as if it were a word complete unto itself.

"Mommy News Network," Xander said. "Look, can I come in or not?"

Willow nodded and went to let him in. A moment later he dropped onto the edge of her bed as she seated herself once more at her computer.

Up close he looked worse, she decided. No, worse

wasn't it, because you had to look bad before you could look worse, and Xander never looked bad to her. But sitting mere feet away from her, signs of fatigue were more clearly drawn. His eyes were bloodshot and his shoulders slumped as he gazed at her. He looked as if he'd aged a few years since the day before.

"How were the movies?" Willow asked.

Rather than answer, Xander asked a question of his own. "Did you hear the news?" he asked. "About Jonathan?"

"Jonathan?" Willow asked. She looked blank. That wasn't someone she thought about very often.

"He's asleep," Xander said. He gave her a quick rundown of the night before, of picking up Jonathan before the movies and dropping him off after. He got that awkward and abashed sound in his voice when he talked about the cheerleader movie and seemed honestly embarrassed to have fallen asleep during it.

"The next thing I knew, Mom was trying to shake me awake," Xander said. "Not that it took much effort. I'd only been out a couple hours."

"She could wake you," Willow said slowly.

Xander nodded.

"But Jonathan was dead to the world," she continued, and immediately regretted her choice of words. Just because she wasn't close to Jonathan didn't mean that she'd ever want anything bad to happen to him. She'd spent plenty of time on the fringes of school society, too much time not to have some sympathy for her low-key classmate.

"Yeah," Xander said. "My mom's ballistic. She's been on the phone all morning, and every time I try to catch some winks, she flips out." He made an expression that looked like a smile but wasn't, not really. "She's been on the phone all day and watching TV, and it's making her crazy. Threw a glass of water at me once," he said. "Dad really got a hoot out of that one. So I cut out."

"Oh," Willow said.

"Just in time, too. She was making noises about having me talk with the police, or public health people," Xander continued. "I don't think that's who needs to be told."

Willow thought again about the search she had run for Buffy into the background and history of the newly reopened drive-in. Was there anything in all those pages of reports that she'd missed? A chill of self-doubt swept through her.

Had she even asked the right questions?

Xander seemed to read her mind. He could do that sometimes. "I don't think it's the movie place, Will," he said. "Or, at least, not *just* the movie place. Mom talked to Aura's folks—"

"Your mother knows Aura's family?" Willow asked, startled. It was hard to think of those two bloodlines interacting, even on a social basis.

"I told you, she's calling *everyone*," Xander said. "But Aura wasn't at the opening."

"I haven't seen her in class lately," Willow said. She rummaged through her memory, looking for the few exchanges she'd had with Cordelia in the previous few days. "Cordy says she's been out of school since Thursday."

"That's because she's been in the hospital since Thursday morning," Xander said. "According to an exclusive report from MNN."

"Sleepy?" Willow asked. A small teddy bear rested on her desktop, next to the computer's docking station. Without conscious thought she picked up the stuffed animal and started to toy with it nervously.

"Very sleepy," Xander said.

"Maybe we should talk to Cordelia about this," Willow said.

"I'll tell you who we should really talk to," Xander said.

"Buffy?"

He nodded again. "And Giles. Cordy may know a lot about penguins, but she's not the brains of the operation," he said. "Any chance I could use the phone?"

"Sure," Willow said. "It's just a matter of deciding who to call first."

She reached for the phone, but it rang before her fingers even made contact. Startled, Willow picked it up before the first ring completed. A brief exchange later, she passed the receiver to Xander, who looked at her blankly.

"Buffy," she said. "She's looking for you."

He looked a lot happier when he took the phone and began talking.

Chapter Nine

Buffy had been to Giles's home many times before. When she knocked on his front door this time, its arched wood sounded precisely as it always had. Even the polished brass of the doorknob, warmed by the midday sun, was reassuringly familiar as she coiled her fingers around it.

Even so, something *felt* different.

She turned to the others lingering behind her. "No answer," she said. "Just like the phone."

That in itself was an ominous sign. Ten calls to Giles's number had produced responses numbering precisely zero. It was Saturday, and there was no reason to expect him to be at home, but it wasn't like him to leave his answering machine unset.

"Car's still here," Xander said. He took up position beside the little, low-powered vehicle. Cars as an institution engaged his attention, even when the example at hand failed to impress. He was a teenage boy, after all. He leaned to peer through one closed car window, shading his view with cupped hands. "Nothing here," he said.

"Here, either," Cordelia said, but she seemed to base her findings on only the most cursory inspection of the courtyard. It was Willow who was still taking the lay of the land, peering behind bushes and eyeing the cut grass.

"Stay out here, guys," Buffy said. She was getting a bad feeling about all this.

"Buff, you shouldn't go in there alone," Xander said. Cordelia and Willow nodded in agreement, but neither girl moved to join Buffy when he did.

"Down, boy," she said, waving him back again. "I need reinforcements on the outside." This time he obeyed and rejoined the others as Buffy knocked on the door one last time. "Hello?" she called loudly. "Giles, if you won't come out, I'm coming in."

Still no answer.

She repeated the command. "Stay out here, all of you. I'll let you know when the coast is clear." She continued more softly as she gripped the knob more tightly, "*If* the coast is clear."

She thought she'd need to break the lock. For someone with Buffy's strength, that kind of thing wasn't particularly difficult. This time, however, it wasn't even necessary. The knob turned easily, another ominous sign. It wasn't like Giles to leave the entrance to his home unsecured. Buffy pushed the door open.

"Hello?" she called. "Giles, it's me. Hello? Hello?"

With one final glance to make sure that the others didn't follow, she stepped into the shadowed interior of her Watcher's domicile. A minute or two later she reemerged and gestured everyone inside.

"C'mon, guys," she said. "See if *you* can figure this out."

"Wow," Willow said less than a minute later, followed by echoes from Xander and Cordelia.

"You see my point?" Buffy said, and closed the front door behind them.

There was nothing wrong with the home, at least nothing that the naked eye could see. The windows were closed and unbroken, and the doors were similarly intact. The furniture had been recently dusted, and the books and magazines laid out on the low coffee table were in neat stacks. The place could have been a film set, or a model home, albeit one lavishly furnished with reading materials.

But Giles himself was nowhere to be found. She'd checked the other rooms. Worse, there was an odd feeling to the air, a faint reminder of the electricity she'd experienced while on patrol the previous nights.

Buffy felt vaguely as if she'd entered a haunted house.

Only one thing seemed overtly amiss: the desk's working surface. Next to open books, age-yellowed documents, and a legal pad, a tea service perched. It had been abandoned while still on the job, and that had clearly been a while ago. The water in the pot was room temperature, and the leaves in the basket filter were soggy and swollen from steeping far too long.

Beside the pot sat a teacup on the same tray. The level of dark tea in it had dropped, leaving a ring to mark its original level, and Buffy could tell from the mark that much of the liquid loss had been to evaporation. The cup had been left unattended for some hours.

Giles had been sitting here, Buffy realized. He'd prepared himself a pot of tea to accompany his review of the books and excursuses.

Before he could finish, it had happened.

Whatever "it" was.

"Very *Marie Celeste*," Willow said. She inspected the tea service daintily and then lifted one of the open books. Her nose wrinkled as she leafed though it.

"Marie who?" Buffy asked her.

"Not a who, a what," Cordelia said, her back to the rest of them. She was busily inspecting a decorative wall hanging that clearly did not meet the elevated Chase family standards. "Crew disappeared, with meals waiting for them on the tables. It's a mystery that's never been solved."

The others stared at her for a silent moment. Xander broke it with a two-word question. "Book report?" he asked.

Cordelia shook her head. "Don't be silly. I saw a movie. That's what this is like, though."

"She's right," Willow said, sounding vaguely distracted. She had begun to read, and the words had drawn her in, but not so deeply that she couldn't kibitz. "It's one of the classic maritime mysteries, and it dates back to the 1870s. Very old school, and it's never been solved."

"This isn't good," Buffy said. "This isn't good at all."

Now Willow looked up from the book. "No," she said. She looked worried. "It isn't."

"What is it, Willow?" Buffy asked. "What did you find?"

"Just—just a story," the other girl said slowly. She tilted the worn book so that the others could see its title.

The worn gilt letters read, *Secrets of Alchemie and How to Profit Thereby,* followed by a subtitle in smaller type too worn to be deciphered.

"You and Giles and your ancient secret texts," Cordelia said, then fell silent as Buffy shot her a glance.

Willow shook her head. "This isn't old," she said. "Not really. Only about a hundred years' vintage—"

"Sounds pretty old to me," Xander said from the kitchen. "Buff, there's tea fixin's laid out in here—you should take a look."

"Later, Xander," Buffy said, but filed the information away in her head. It comported with what she'd already determined, that someone or something had taken Giles by surprise. "What's special about the book?" she asked Willow.

"Nothing, really," Willow said. "That's what's weird." When the others stared at her, she took a deep breath before continuing. "I mean, Giles has quite the library, you know. He's got books bound in demon-hide and printed on skin, and he's got books that I swear are older than people, even though I know that makes no sense at—"

"Willow," Buffy said. "Focus."

The red-haired girl nodded. She sat in the desk chair and set the book down, still open, as she continued. "This is nothing special," she said. "It's not very old, and—"

"A hundred years," Xander said again. He'd emerged from the kitchen and was standing in the doorway.

"Not very old by Giles's standards," Willow said, continuing on. "And this is a popular work." She paused. "Not bestseller popular, but aimed at a general audience."

"A *Reader's Digest* condensed occult text?" Buffy asked, feeling faintly boggled. What was next? A paperback edition of *The Crimson Chronicles*?

Willow nodded again. "Kinda," she said, turning pages. "More like an overview with pretty pictures. You could sell this down at the Magic Box and not worry about anyone losing his soul in the process. I'm surprised Giles even had something like this."

"He said he wanted to figure out what was in the missing books," Buffy said slowly. Her forehead wrinkled as she thought. "He wanted to extradite—"

"Extrapolate, probably," Willow said. She gave a faint smile. When Willow made corrections, she was far gentler about it than Cordelia.

"Extrapolate," Buffy said, more sharply than she'd intended. No matter who was doing it, he didn't like being corrected.

"Uh-huh," Willow said. She started to read. "Give me a minute. I've done enough research with Giles that I know how his methods. Maybe I can figure out what he was working on." She paused again. "Specifically, I mean."

Buffy gave her the moment. To pass the time, she accepted Xander's invitation to inspect the kitchen. He'd been right. The work area was what she termed a tidy mess: kettle still half-full, whistle top set aside. The tea-leaf tin was tightly closed but remained on the counter, rather than in the cupboard where she knew it belonged. An insulated pot holder lay beside it, along with the spring-loaded tongs that she'd seen Giles use to fill the teapot's basket filter.

Looking at the array made her feel worse. For some reason the tableau acted as a focus for the worry and presentiment she felt. She'd known Giles only a year or so, but that year had been filled with challenge and adventure. Though she'd have a hard time admitting it to anyone, he'd become more than a friend and a mentor. No one could ever fill the gap left by her absent father, but Giles's presence made the void somewhat less consuming.

And now someone or something had taken him from her.

"He was here," she said very softly. "He must have been working on the missing book thing." She tapped the working surface with one finger. "And they got him."

"Got him?" Xander said, still at her side. "I mean, are you sure he didn't just pop off to the market or something?" But his question had the hopeful quality of someone grasping at straws.

Buffy shook her head. In her world there were no

"rational explanations," no pat assemblies of fact and circumstance that could explain a situation like this. Even worst-case scenarios were almost never bad enough.

"And leave the door unlocked?" Buffy asked. Taking things in context, that seemed even more conclusive than the abandoned tea service. Giles spent countless hours impressing upon her the need for personal security. She couldn't imagine him not locking his own front door.

"No signs of a struggle," Xander said. He looked very worried now, more worried than she would have expected.

Perversely, though, she found some hope in his words. Xander had a keen grasp of the obvious, and sometimes obvious was good. There was, indeed, no sign of a struggle: no broken furniture, no spilled tea, no sign of damage to doors or windows. Best of all, no blood trace lingered. Wherever Giles had gone, he'd gone there uninjured.

That could change, of course, but for now, she clung to the hope.

"He boiled water and he brewed tea," she said slowly, thinking things through. She walked back into the living area and stood behind the desk, nodding at Willow before she continued. "He likes tea in the evenings. Says it helps him think clearly. He was working on the missing book thing."

Willow was buried in her review now, looking from open book to legal pad and back again. She offered not even a nod of acknowledgment in response.

"Uh-huh. And then someone knocked on the door," Buffy said. It was the only conclusion that made sense. Giles had gone to receive a visitor, only the visitor had received him instead. "Let's take another look outside."

Cordelia rolled her eyes slightly but accompanied Buffy and Xander outside. After the ominously empty interior of Giles's home, the afternoon sun felt good, and the air seemed fresh and clean. Even so, the open door and empty windows were haunting reminders that Giles had gone missing. Buffy tried to think of other things as she and the others took another, closer look for some indication of the night's events.

Xander hung close to Buffy after they'd exited. Even when Buffy told Cordelia that she was going to do a quick perimeter search, Xander fell in beside her, ignoring her suggestion that he inspect the driveway area a second time. Although the Slayer was accustomed to her friend's attentiveness, she was equally accustomed to being obeyed. His hovering struck her as being out of the norm.

"Xander," she said. "He's going to be all right."

"Huh?" Xander asked. The concern on his features was even more evident in the daylight.

"Giles," Buffy said. She forced herself to sound confident as they rounded the corner of the building. A small utility shed bordered on the courtyard, and she gave it a quick inspection. "He's pretty tough, really, and he knows how to fight. We didn't find any blood, so—"

"I'm not worried about Giles," Xander said.

"Why not?" Buffy asked sharply. The shed was securely locked. Xander's dismissal of Giles's situation irritated her.

"Not like that," he said, raising his hands as if to ward off an attack. "I like G just fine, you know that. But like you said, he's a pro. We'll find him and he'll be okay. Really. I'm sure."

"Then spill," Buffy said, still reconnoitering. The shrubbery that framed one window was intact and undisturbed.

"It's Jonathan," Xander said. "He went to the movies with me last night and he fell asleep."

"Well, c'mon, Xander," Buffy said. Genuine irritation cut through the generalized worry she felt. Her friend's priorities seemed a trifle misplaced. "They were just old movies," she said.

"That's not what I mean, Buffy," Xander said. "I mean, he's *still* asleep—"

"Xander, you were out all night," Buffy interrupted. "I mean, you look beat even now, and—"

"No," he said forcefully. "His parents found him on the living room floor, sound asleep, and *they can't wake him up*."

Buffy paused in midstride. She looked at her friend. "Okay," she said. "I said it before and I'll say it again. Spill."

Xander spilled. In sentences that were surprisingly precise and succinct, he recounted for Buffy the previous night's adventures. He told her about borrowing his parents' car and picking up Jonathan. He offered summaries of the four movies they'd more-or-less watched and, remarkably, the summaries were short enough not to be annoying. He told her about the ride home and dropping Jonathan off at the Levenson house and going home himself.

"The next thing I know, Mom's flipping out," he said. "I scrammed. That's why I was with Willow when you called."

One thing that Buffy always liked about Xander was his overall good cheer, something that seemed intrinsic to his personality. Seeing him the way he was now, worried, fretful, and deeply, deeply concerned, was always jarring. She realized with a pang that she'd half-hoped he could provide her with reassurance, only to find the shoe on the other foot.

He wanted her to make things better, and Buffy knew that right now she couldn't.

"Xander," she said. "I'm sure everything's fine. He was out all night, he got sleepy—"

"Buffy, he's in the *hospital*," Xander said. "The doctors can't wake him up either. They're not calling it a coma, but there's something wrong with him, seriously wrong."

"It—it's not your fault," was all she could think to say. "You said that Aura was sick too, and—"

"I don't *care* about Aura," Xander interrupted again. He paused. "No, I don't mean that. It's just, Jonathan was with me—"

"Hey! There you are!" said Cordelia, sounding sharp and demanding as she came around a corner. Rather than continue, however, she eyed Buffy and Xander with what the Slayer could have sworn was suspicion.

Buffy sighed. Giles's absence was a more pressing issue than Jonathan Levenson's excessive drowsiness; Xander was just going to have to accept that. Besides, work was the best medicine sometimes. Once Xander got busy, he'd feel better.

"What is it *now*?" she asked.

Cordelia led them to her find. In a grassy patch, she knelt and pointed. "Look," she said.

Scarring the soft earth were a series of half-moon divots. Each was about the size of a large man's hand, and each dug deeply enough to tear grass aside and reveal the soil beneath. When she probed one cut with her index finger, Buffy could see that the gouge was mid-knuckle deep.

Buffy looked at her blankly. She couldn't find it in herself to be entirely pleased that Cordelia had made the discovery—any discovery.

"They're hoofprints," Cordelia said, as if it were the most obvious thing in the world.

"Oh," Buffy said, nonplussed. To her, hooves and hoofprints meant one thing. "You mean, like, hairy goat-legged demon hooves?"

"Don't be ridiculous," Cordelia said. She was looking closely at the prints, estimating the distance between them, busily demonstrating more expertise that was nearly as unwelcome as it was surprising. "These are *way* too big for a goat. These were made by a horse, a big one." She moved over to the walkway and pointed. "Here," she said. "Look."

More half-moon marks showed on the flagstones. They were bright scars on the gray stone, faint but undeniable. They were the marks that a horse's steel shoes would make on stone. Buffy eyed them. Clearly, Cordelia was right again.

Xander asked the question she wanted answered. "Cordy," he said, "what's with all the data points lately? You taking smart-girl pills or something?"

The taller girl shot him a withering glance. What Cordelia regarded as the famous Chase charm was in full bloom now. Most would have mistaken it for arrogance and hauteur, and Buffy wasn't at all sure they wouldn't have been right. Reluctantly, however, she decided that Cordelia had the right to be proud of herself.

For today, anyway.

"Don't be silly," snapped the Queen of Sunnydale High. "I told you before, I'm not stupid."

With that particular genius inherent in the human male, Xander dug the hole deeper. "But the *Marie Celeste* thing," he said. "And now this horse business—"

"Xander, hello!" Cordelia said, thoroughly peeved by the implied slight. The midday sun made her chestnut hair even more lustrous. "I'm not just not stupid. My family's rich, remember?"

"Uh, yeah," Xander said. "And your point is . . . ?"

"And what is it that rich families do at exclusive resorts?" Cordelia asked. "Some families, at some resorts, that is. Hint: We wear jodhpurs."

"Um," Xander said slowly. "Horseback riding?"

She nodded. Despite the unnerving situation, Buffy and Xander flashed brief smiles. There was something very satisfying about seeing Cordelia so thoroughly in her element.

"Okay," Buffy said. She massaged her temples, hoping to stimulate thought. "Someone got Giles and spirited him away on horseback. Maybe a cowboy."

"A . . . cowboy?" Xander said very slowly.

"Hey!" Willow called to them from the doorway. "I think I've found something!"

"—mysterious disorder that has claimed more than thirty local victims," the newscaster said. She was a youngish woman, no older than her early thirties, Asian, and with a good voice. She had skin the color of old ivory and her dark hair was short and neatly styled so that it looked like a tight black helmet. Joyce Summers had seen her work before, and knew that she was good at her job.

The newscaster continued, *"Earlier this hour we talked with a hospital spokesperson who offered a tentative theory on why some of our young people just won't wake up. Now, in response to those comments, I'd like welcome to our program a newcomer to our city, the proprietor of the newly reopened Sunnydale Drive-In."*

The camera pulled back into a two-shot, revealing the ballyhooed guest seated across the round table that was pretty much a standard fixture on local-market news and commentary programs. Even viewed through the camera's unblinking eye, the man had an immediacy and magnetism about him that Joyce found fascinating. He wore an Armani suit, and his iron-colored hair and beard were impeccably styled. His smile appeared to be directed at her and her alone. Joyce liked him instantly.

"*Welcome to KRAD News at Noon, Mr. Belasimo,*" the newscaster said.

The guest winced very faintly at the sound of his name, and Joyce was certain that the newscaster had mispronounced it, but he didn't correct her. Instead, in a voice as warm and smooth as melted butter, he said, "*Thank you, Ms. Hasbro. I'm very happy to be here in this lovely city, and in the presence of such a charming hostess.*"

Hasbro's professional demeanor broke, and she giggled. She waved one hand in dismissal and smiled again. "*The pleasure is all mine, I assure you, sir,*" she said. "*And please, it's Enola.*" She became more businesslike as she addressed the camera. "*Mr. Belasimo is a newcomer to our community. The Sunnydale Drive-In ran its first programming in more than twenty years last night.*"

"*That's correct, Enola,*" Balsamo said genially. "*Although I feel constrained to point out that the movies we're running are at least that old themselves. For our inaugural exhibition, we chose to present a festival of vintage drive-in fare.*"

Joyce, still watching, was suddenly all too aware that she was alone in the house and alone on the big sofa that offered the best view of the Summers family television. She spent a lot of time alone these days. She felt sudden envy for Hasbro, who had so much of her life ahead of her and whose work put her in close proximity to newsworthy movers and shakers. She knew that the emotion was absurd, but it was undeniable, too. She'd been alone so often lately, since Buffy's father had left, and Buffy's life had become so busy. Now, on such a beautiful day, she sat by herself and watched television.

Why was that? It wasn't the kind of question that Joyce allowed herself to ask very often.

Hasbro continued, *"We spoke in the last hour with Dr. Orloff, who's treating many of the victims of this sleeping sickness—"*

"So-called sleeping sickness," Balsamo said with an indulgent chuckle. It was an interruption, but the trim and attractive newscaster didn't seem to mind. *"I've been following the coverage, as you might imagine."*

"So-called sleeping sickness, then," Hasbro conceded with a smile. *"Dr. Orloff mentioned the fact that the majority of the thirty individuals currently being treated had attended the grand reopening last night of the Sunnydale Drive-In. He speculated that some form of food poisoning might be at work."*

Balsamo looked annoyed. Joyce sympathized. He was a businessman, after all, and had every right to be concerned about protecting his investment. *"I don't believe that Dr. Orloff's comments were appropriate,"* he said. *"At the very least, they were ill-considered. Representatives of my organization have been in contact with the hospital administration about this. Believe me, before reopening, the theater concession stand was thoroughly inspected. We comply fully with all health code standards."*

Joyce believed him. She believed him as thoroughly as she believed that the sun rose in the east and set in the west. Something about this gentleman commanded utter confidence in the words he spoke. Joyce hoped that Hasbro would just shut up and let the man speak.

Hasbro didn't. She persevered, with words that challenged, even if her tone of voice did not. *"But surely, Mr. Belasimo, the fact that twenty-seven of thirty victims have been verified as having attended—"*

"Precisely, Ms. Hasbro," Balsamo said. The use of her surname made the newscaster wince. *"At least three of the victims of this so-called illness have no connection whatsoever with my theater."* He smiled, and Joyce's world became a warmer, more welcoming place. *"Really, Enola, do I appear to be someone who would continue operations if there was the slightest chance that the innocent could come to harm?"*

Hasbro smiled ruefully, clearly impressed by the line of reasoning. *"No,"* she said. *"No, of course not."*

"Excellent," Balsamo said. His smile widened, and sparks seemed to dance in his eyes. *"In fact, I'd like to issue a special invitation,"* he said. *"For tonight, and tonight only, the Sunnydale Drive-In will waive its quite reasonable admission charge."* The camera zoomed closer, until Balsamo's face nearly filled the screen. *"So, if any of your viewers are fans of classic drive-in fare, or if they simply enjoy a corking good yarn, I invite them to attend tonight. It's my treat. I think I can promise you an experience like no other."*

The phone rang as Hasbro commenced her closing

comments. Joyce let it ring a few times, waiting to answer it until she was sure that Balsamo would have nothing more to say. By the seventh ring Hasbro and her guest alike had been supplanted by an irritated-looking man in a white lab coat. A caption identified him as Dr. Orloff, presumably making some sort of rebuttal. She ignored him and lifted the receiver at last.

It was Barney.

"Oh, hello," Joyce said, once the bank official had identified himself. "No, no, I'm not busy at all." She paused and listened. "Are you sure that's a good idea?" she asked. Then, after another pause, she smiled. "No, Barney, I'm not busy tonight either," she said. "I think that's a nice idea. We could have fun."

"Do you all remember when Giles asked about ectoplasm?" Willow asked. Seated at the Watcher's desk, open books and notes at her fingertips, she waited for an answer. With Giles among the missing, Willow was pretty much the next best thing they had to a watcher, since she'd assisted him so many times in his research. Now she was thoroughly in her element as the substitute fount of all knowledge. Dire as the situation might be, it was clear that she enjoyed the role fate had thrust upon her.

Cordelia, seated on the couch with the others, paid reasonable attention. She knew all too well that Willow was smarter than she was, or at least more knowledgeable. Recognizing that superiority was a tough pill to swallow; Cordelia consoled herself with the fact that the little brainiac's expertise ran to useless stuff like computer programming and ancient history. She didn't know a darned thing about basic fashion principles or what style might have made her stubby little legs look longer. No, the kind of things that Willow knew were useful in high school and monster hunting, and Cordy fully intended to leave both behind after graduating.

"Cordy?" Willow asked. "We're waiting."

Cordelia checked to see if she'd raised her hand, by some dumb conditioned reflex. She hadn't, and said as much.

"Aw c'mon, Cordy, play along," Xander said on her left.

Without being invited, he had plopped himself on the center cushion of the couch, between Cordy and Buffy. No doubt Xander thought he'd nabbed the cat-bird seat, but all he'd really done was make it easy for Cordelia to give him a quick elbow in the ribs. She did so, and he gasped.

"I'd like this to be a demilitarized zone," he said weakly.

"I'll demilitarize you," she muttered from the corner of her mouth. More loudly, she continued, "It's what ghosts are made out of."

"Very good," Willow said, with a smile and a nod. "You deserve a gold star, young lady! If I had any to give, that is."

"Willow," Buffy said. The edge in her voice made the name a warning.

"Um, yes," Willow said. "Well, ectoplasm is more than that, really. It's uh, um, the underlying psycho-etheric constitutional substance of an individual's soul, spirit, or *atman*." She spoke the string of words in a singsong voice that suggested they were memorized, and recently memorized, at that. As if to confirm, she glanced at a sheet of Giles's notes. "Gold star for me, too," she said softly.

"Uh-huh." The two syllables could have come from any of the couch potatoes, or all of them. They were the kind of almost meaningless syllables so often used by students to indicate acknowledgment, if not understanding.

Cordelia could feel her eyes starting to glaze over. Giles was pretty nice for a guy who'd been around almost as long as fire, and she certainly wished him well, but life went on. She wondered who was playing at the Bronze tonight.

Not Willow, though. Such trivial issues were clearly long miles from the other girl's mind as she warmed to her subject. "Now, according to his notes, that's what Giles was researching," Willow said. "Or, it's what the missing books were about. Ectoplasm and its practical applications." She held up another book, presenting its cover. The words read, *Psychic Humours and Their Uses*.

"A joke book?" Xander asked, then coughed as Cordelia elbowed him again.

"It's another word for 'fluid,'" Willow said. "There's bunches of terms for this stuff. Psycho-etheric fluxes, psychomatter, ectoplasm, more."

"None of that sounds like magick, Will," Buffy said.

Willow nodded, looking genuinely and completely

pleased for the first time in a while. Her happiness at Buffy's question pushed aside her worries about Giles, at least for the moment. "Very good, Buffy!" she said. "A gold—"

Buffy executed a short, emphatic shake of her head. Between that and the serious expression the Slayer wore, her message was clear. This was no time for role-playing or banter.

"It doesn't sound like magick because it's not," Willow said. She indicated once more the books that Giles had left behind. "Most of this stuff is what you'd call proto-science."

"Proto-science?" Cordelia asked. She gave voice to the question without conscious thought. Willow's term sounded so odd that it demanded explanation.

"Yeah," Willow said. She set the book aside and raised something else. It was some sort of plastic envelope, thick and rigid but transparent, so that its contents were revealed. Those contents seemed much more typical of Giles's Watcher archives. They were sheets of something that might have been paper, but which Cordelia knew intuitively was not. It seemed to wiggle slightly in the envelope, as if alive. Whatever the stuff was, it was browned and tattered by age, and covered with diagrams and runes that Cordelia knew she never could have read, not even if her life depended on it. That kind of stuff was Greek to her, and was likely Greek to the Greeks, too. Of course, if it was Greek to Greeks that would mean . . .

Cordelia tried to focus on Willow's mini-lecture.

"*This* is magick," Willow said. She tapped her

finger on the envelope, making a popping noise, then set it down. She gestured at the books. "These are proto-sciences. Alchemy, spiritualism, mesmerism, phrenology—well, that last one's more of a pseudo-science, really."

She went on to explain in more detail. According to Willow, magick was primarily an art, one that relied heavily on an individual's aptitudes and the invocation of superhuman entities such as gods and demons. Science worked differently. Scientists gathered data and built hypotheses that could be tested by experimentation, and relied on known physical forces and circumstances. Magick was as old as or older than mankind, depending on the definition. Science and the scientific method were much younger, dating back to about the Renaissance, filtering out into the general culture in the ensuing decades and centuries.

"That's the Cliff's Notes version, at least," she said. "It's messier than that."

"Science good, magick bad," Xander said, boiling it down further.

"No," Willow said. She picked up the plastic-clad document and shook her head. "No, not at all. They're different ways of dealing with the universe, and they overlapped for a while. They still have a lot in common. Why, some assembler language commands are an awful lot like incantations, and—"

"Cut to the chase, Willow, please," Buffy said. "What does *any* of this have to do with our kidnapping cowboy?"

"Cowboy?"

"I'll tell you later," the Slayer promised. "You said you think you found something. Tell us what."

"Two somethings, really," Willow said. She pointed at Giles's legal pad, the canary yellow sheets covered with notes in the Englishman's neat handwriting. "Giles uses a lot of abbreviations here and he wrote *around* a lot of stuff instead of *about* it, but as near as I can tell, he was zeroing in on the proto-sciences. Those were early mixtures of science and magic. Stuff like alchemy. That's the old version of chemistry, all mixed up with astrology and spiritualism and other stuff. Alchemists were heavy into the eternal mysteries—how to live forever, how to turn lead to gold, that kind of thing."

"I know about alchemy," Buffy said darkly. She'd seen a lot of things in her tenure as the Slayer. "It's not good stuff."

"Maybe not . . . but it's what Giles was looking into," Willow said.

She flipped through the notepad and found a particularly busy page, dense with occult-looking symbols and diagrams. Giles had made abbreviated sketches of the twelve signs of the zodiac, with arrows leading from one to another. Some lines of text were so small that even Cordelia's vision, excellent for distance, couldn't make them out completely. There were exceptions, though. Giles had made lists of terms. At their heads, in larger lettering, were words like "Ectoplasm," "Psycho-Etherics," "Astral Projection," and "Elemental Phases."

"So we're looking for an alchemist," Xander said.

"Maybe," Willow said.

Without asking permission, Xander half-stood and claimed one of the books, then settled back into his seat. He opened the volume and flipped through its pages. "Hey," he said, pleased. "This is in English! I can read this!" He paused. "Sort of."

Cordelia craned her neck and snuck a peek. She could see what he meant. Even setting issues of language aside, many of Giles's books were physically difficult to read, with ornate lettering and time-faded inks. This one, presumably because it was a much younger work, was a different matter. Its pages were worn and marked from handling, but only slightly yellowed with age. The text that adorned them was typeset rather than hand-illuminated, but the lines of type were uneven and had ragged margins. Worse, the text was in English, but only sort of. It seemed to Cordelia that every fifth word was misspelled or improperly capitalized.

"Jeezy-peezy," she said. "Didn't they ever hear of spell-check?"

Xander shrugged. Despite the urgency of the situation, he seemed oddly preoccupied, or even bored. He flipped though the pages more quickly, pausing only to eye illustrations, of which there were many. With each turned page, the musty aroma of old paper scented the air.

"You said you found two somethings, Willow," Buffy said. Her words were less a reminder than they were a prompt to continue, and her voice held a note of command that Cordelia had heard before. Willow might think that she was running the improvised lecture session, but it was the Slayer who was boss.

"Yeah," Willow said. She lifted two of the plastic-clad documents she'd toyed with earlier, and extended one each in Cordelia's and Buffy's directions. "These are excursuses," she said.

"Curses?!" Cordelia nearly yelped the word and pulled back the hand she'd reflexively extended.

"No, *ex*cursuses," Willow said. Without waiting to be asked, she provided the definition. "Detailed discussions of topics addressed in an academic work."

"Sort of a super-footnote, Cordy," Buffy said. "Giles and I talked about them earlier."

"What do they say, then?" Cordelia asked, still not accepting the proffered item. Something about the way the thing looked made her feel all squirmy.

"Well, as near as I can tell, this one's mostly about astral projection," Willow said. "I can't be sure, though, because it's in a dead language, and all I can puzzle out are some symbols. The second one's in some kind of debased Latin, and its some kind of treatise on ectoplasm and spiritual regeneration. I can't make any sense out of the others, but none of them looks like good news."

Cordelia didn't like the sound of that. It was another thing she'd never admit to anyone who mattered, but she didn't like it at all when Willow expressed ignorance about things pertaining to slayage. Such comments were bad signs in the best of times, and made worse now by the absence of Giles.

Her earlier boredom was completely gone now, and she waited to see what came next.

"Hey!" Xander said sharply. "Hey! I know this guy!"

He'd opened the alchemy book to an illustration. It was printed on paper better than the pages that flanked it, and looked to be some kind of steel-plate engraving, like the faces on currency. It showed an aristocratic-looking man in old-fashioned breeches and jacket. He had broad features, muttonchop whiskers, and a powdered wig, resembling someone who might have stepped off a dollar bill. Cordelia took all of that in with a glance, but took little real notice. Her attention was drawn by the man's eyes.

Whoever the anonymous artist had been, he'd known his craft. The man's eyes were deep-set and shadowed, but, paradoxically, they seemed lit by an inner intensity. Even across the gulf of years, even filtered through an artist's sensibilities and the process of book production, Cordelia found them oddly compelling. They had magnetism that drew her attention and held it.

A caption identified the image as being of one Count Alessandro di Cagliostro.

"You don't know him," Willow said. "He's been dead for two hundred years."

"Oh, like *that's* a problem," Xander said. They'd met plenty of dead people in the previous year or so. "I'm sure of it. Here, I'll show you," he said, and drew a ballpoint from his pocket to amend the illustration.

There came a yelping sound as Willow protested. Rather than let him deface the book, she rooted though

Giles's desk drawers and found a piece of tracing paper. Xander shook his head but complied. Positioning the sheet, he used quick, short pen-strokes to add a beard to Cagliostro.

"There," Xander said. "Mr. Balsamo. You could put that on his driver's license."

"Balsamo?" Cordelia asked. She'd never heard the name before.

"Balsamo?" Willow said. "Are you serious, Xander?"

"Boss-man at the drive-in," Xander said. He closed the book angrily and turned to Buffy. "See?" he said. "I told you I got Jonathan into this. I told you it's my fault."

"Now, hold on," Buffy started. "There's more to this than—"

"Who's Balsamo?" Cordelia asked.

"Guiseppe Balsamo," Willow said, as if that explained everything.

It didn't, of course.

"Dammit, I know what I did," Xander said. His voice was thick, and the usual joking quality in his words was missing entirely. "I did it to him, and to Aura, and to all the rest. I was part of this, somehow."

"Aura?" Cordelia asked. She liked to think of herself as quick on her feet, conversation-wise, but the questions and answers were coming entirely too fast. She was getting lost. It seemed like everyone was talking at once, and about different things.

"Aura's in the hospital, Cordy," Buffy said with a sidelong glance. "So are a lot of people. Some kind of sleeping sickness."

"Cagliostro was some kind of supermojo alchemist back in the eighteenth century," Willow said. "Depending on who you talk to, Balsamo might have been his real name."

"Aura wasn't at the drive-in, was she?" Buffy asked Xander.

"Does the drive-in sound like Aura?" Xander responded.

"STOP IT! ALL OF YOU, STOP TALKING RIGHT NOW!" Cordelia shouted, as loud as the loudest cheer in the most contested football game. Her words were like thunder in the living room's confines.

The others were stunned, but complied. They fell silent and looked at her blankly. While they waited, she took a deep breath and gathered her thoughts. Finally, she continued. "You," she said, pointing at Xander. "Tell me what happened to Aura." She paused. "And Jonathan, I guess." She pointed at Buffy. "You tell me about this sleeping sickness," she said. "Willow gets Cagliostro."

Surprisingly, all three of them nodded obediently. Perhaps less surprisingly, they all began to speak at precisely the same time. Cordelia had to do some more shouting and issue some more orders before they fell into line, and filled her in on their respective areas of (relative) expertise. When they finished, she took another deep breath and sorted through the flood of information.

"Okay," she said. "Aura's in the hospital and no one thought to tell me, thank you very much. There's, like, a whole bunch of people in town who won't wake up."

Buffy and Xander nodded again. Buffy, especially, seemed bemused by the demands for information, but that was fine with Cordelia. It was about time someone started thinking about this stuff clearly.

"Most of those thirty were at the drive-in last night," Cordelia continued, "which is being run by some Penn and Teller type who died three hundred years ago. That doesn't sound very likely, does it?"

"Alchemist," Willow said meekly. "Those guys are illusionists, and he was an alchemist. And he only died about two hundred years ago. If it's him." She explained that Count Cagliostro was actually quite a shadowy figure, historically speaking. He'd used many names, and his death had been reported more than once. Even the identification of his real name as Guiseppe Balsamo seemed not to be certain.

"Close enough," Cordelia said. "Now, what do we do next?"

"We?" Buffy asked. "I'm heading out to the drive-in, and I'm going to turn this guy inside out and mail him to Antarctica."

Xander shook his head. He looked worried, worried enough that Cordelia felt concern. Certainly, even in her experience, Xander had involved himself in some pretty outrageous situations, but he rarely involved others. She knew that Xander was a lot more compassionate than most people realized, even if he didn't show it very often.

"That won't work," he said. "There's nothing out there in daylight. I don't know where the boss—where this guy hangs out in the daytime, but it's not there."

"Maybe we could find him," Willow said slowly. "Giles made some notes about tracking spells, and there's something about crystals—"

"Magick?" Buffy asked.

Willow nodded.

Buffy shook her head. "You've been a big help already," she said. "But I don't think you're ready to actually try a spell. Let's consider other options."

"There's always more research," Willow said. She looked thoughtful. "In fact, I'd like to look into this drive-in thing a bit more."

"Angel checked the place out," Buffy said. "So did you, for that matter."

"I don't think I asked the right questions, though," Willow said slowly. "This sleeping sickness business gives me an idea."

Buffy gestured at the crowded bookcases that lined much of Giles's living room. "Go wild," she said. "I'm sure Giles won't mind.

"Actually, the idea I have, I don' t think these can help me with."

"There's more upstairs, and I might be able to figure out a way to get us into the school."

"No," Willow said. "I was thinking more like the public library. They have bound newspapers there."

"Okay, then," Buffy said. She stood. "Let's go."

"Not me, Buff," Xander said. His words were surprising. "I'm not going with you. Not right now at least."

"Why not?" Buffy asked. Her tone was sharp, but she looked puzzled. Cordelia knew why. Given his head, Xander would spend most of his waking hours as Buffy's shadow. "You've got better plans? We really need your help, Xander."

He shrugged. "Not for this part. Willow can research rings around me," he said. "I want to go to the hospital and check up on Jonathan."

Chapter Ten

For Giles the world came back into focus very slowly. It was a far less pleasant world than the one he'd left behind. Gone were the cradling support of his desk chair and the welcome, musty scent of old books. Instead he felt hard ceramic, cool and slick against his skin, and his nostrils flared with the astringent scent of cleaning compounds. Bright lights shone down on him from above, and the first thing he could see as his vision cleared was a network of white grout lines, separating squares of bright color that had been buffed to a high gloss.

He was on a foreign floor. His last memories were of opening his front door to a stranger.

With some effort he struggled to his feet. Reality resolved itself a bit more, and he realized that he was in a washroom. He tottered to the sink and ran water to splash on his face. The cold wetness felt good. Above the sink was a mirror. His glasses lay on the wash-stand. He donned them and returned his attention to the mirror, inspecting himself for damage.

He didn't find any. That in itself was worth noting. Giles had lived an interesting life—rather more inter-esting than most watchers, actually—and he'd been knocked unconscious more than a few times over the years.

There was no blood, no bruising. Now that he was awake, he realized that there was no headache, either. Even the sour taste that usually accompanied knockout gas or chemical tranquilizers was lacking. The world had gone away, and then it had come back, without injury or incident between. He felt more as if he'd been turned off, like an electrical appliance, and then turned back on again.

It wasn't a good feeling. He didn't care for the idea that someone could do something like that.

Suddenly there came a gritting mechanical sound as a key entered a lock and turned, and then a thunk as a bolt slid back. Giles turned just in time to see the washroom door open.

"Awake, I see," said the man who stood framed in the doorway. "Good."

He looked vaguely familiar, enough so that Giles was certain he'd seen him before. The man was of average height and build, but his stance and posture suggested that he was very physically fit. His hair and beard were both neatly trimmed and styled, both the color of old iron, dark gray verging on black. In one hand was a paper sack that bore a familiar logo, and in the other was a glittering disk of crystal. He'd left the keys dangling in the lock.

"'Good' is not the word I would use," Giles said dryly. He eyed the open doorway. "Who are you and why have you done this?"

The man nodded and raised the disk. "Please, don't make any attempt at escape," he said. "I assure you, it would be futile."

Trying not to be obvious, Giles studied the piece of crystal. From a distance it seemed perfectly transparent, its surface ground and polished to a smooth curve. A ring of brass surrounded it, plain under the man's finger-tips. It was evident from how he handled it that the disk was some manner of weapon, or an object of power.

No, Giles realized suddenly, it wasn't a disk. It was a lens.

"Here you are," the man said, and handed Giles the paper sack. "A late lunch. I know what it's like to be hungry."

Giles didn't think he could eat, but when he opened the bag, the aroma of fried food rushed out and he realized that he was famished. Even so, he set the fast-food meal on the washstand without further examination.

"It's perfectly wholesome," the familiar-looking man said. "Wholesome by colonial standards, at least." He paused. "I owe you an apology, I suppose. Perhaps several."

"Well, never let it be said that I'm not a forgiving sort," Giles said. "If I can just trouble you for a ride back to my residence—"

The man shook his head. "It's not that simple, I'm afraid," he said. There was nothing of menace in his voice, and he spoke with great culture and style. Perversely, Giles found himself warming to the man. He seemed immensely likeable. "It's too late for that. But if I'd realized that this city was home to a watcher, I might well have pursued other opportunities, or undertaken things here differently. It's too late for that, however."

He knew about watchers, and presumably about the Slayer, as well. As such things went, the Watchers Council, its reason for being and its operations, weren't terribly secret, but neither were they common knowledge. The fact that his host knew of them said something of the man's nature, and of the circles in which he likely moved.

"Do I know you?" Giles asked. Sometimes it was best to be direct. The sense of familiarity still gnawed.

"No," the man said with a head shake. "You may know *of* me, however. We're colleagues, of a sort."

"You seem like a civilized sort," Giles said. "This is terribly awkward. Could I at least have your name?"

His host laughed. Like his voice, the sound was warm and rich. "I think not," he said, still chuckling. "We both know that giving one's name is to give power over one's self."

"That's true in only a limited, technical sense," Giles said dismissively. It was curiously refreshing to speak with someone who knew of such things and was willing to treat them seriously. "On a personal level—"

"If I give you my name, you'll know who I am,"

the man said. He didn't laugh this time, but he smiled, revealing perfect teeth. His eyes twinkled. "That's more power than I care to give you, Mr. Giles."

"Oh," the Watcher responded. "Of course." With slight chagrin he reminded himself that this was a captor-captive situation, however politely staged, and not a discussion between learned colleagues. The man's personal magnetism was undeniable, however, and it took conscious effort to resist. "What comes next, then?"

"You'll stay here for a bit," the man said. "After that I'm not sure."

"Hostage?" Giles asked. "I warn you. Experience is that I don't make a very good one."

"Perhaps not," came the reply. "But I've always found it wise to deprive an enemy army of its general. I rather fancy that your Slayer will be less inclined to interfere, absent your guidance."

Giles managed a laugh. It echoed hollowly against the washroom's hard surfaces. One thing he knew with grim certainty was that Buffy would never hesitate to act in his absence. Whether she would act wisely or not was another question altogether. Buffy was, in so many ways, completely unlike any other slayer who had come before her.

"I'll have to tell her you said that," Giles said. "She'll be quite amused."

That netted him another nod. "I'm going to leave you here for now," his host said. "Forgive the accommodations, but security, in this instance, is a more pressing concern than comfort. I'm sure you understand."

"Quite."

"Eat or don't eat," the man said. "It matters not to me. But attempt to escape or send for help in any manner, and I assure you, you'll be stopped. These quarters are quite secure, and I've taken other safeguards beyond walls and locks."

The door closed and the bolt slid home again. Giles made a quick inspection of the washroom and learned approximately what he had expected: The door was heavy and the walls were thick, and there was no window. The entire place was quite solid, however, clean and in excellent repair; presumably, it had been built or renovated only recently. The only way out was through the door, and going through the door meant going through the presumed guard outside as well. Without a weapon of any sort, he was at an extreme disadvantage.

For lack of anything better to do, he perched on the washstand and took inventory of the food bag. It looked beastly: deep-fried trash food of the sort that Americans devoured with such gusto. Even so, his own words to Buffy about blood sugar applied to him as well, so he selected the least of available evils. It was an ominous-looking thing that purported to be a fish sandwich. He began to eat. It was with his third bite that Giles remembered where he'd seen his captor's face before.

It had been in the pages of a book.

Sunnydale had a history; there had been settlements on its site for hundreds of years. It was an old city, by

California standards, and the public library's holdings were impressive evidence of the long years that it had been in operation. The upper levels of the library were modern, nicely designed and brightly lit, but the lower levels were darker and more claustrophobic. That was where management stored the old books, the ones that almost no one ever asked for, but that were worth keeping for their historical or archival value. It was also where the bound periodical collection lived, thick volumes of aging paper that bowed the shelves. Each pseudo-leather spine was labeled in stenciled gilt letters, presenting title and dates, and volume and issue numbers.

Buffy and Willow were there now, the sole occupants of a reading room. After Willow's fifth request for old newspapers, the librarian on duty had given up. She had led them to the long-term storage area—usually off-limits to browsers—explained how the file system worked, and left them to their own devices.

"See?" Willow asked. Her hair was mussed and her skin shiny with perspiration, but she seemed quite pleased with herself. "There's plenty of stuff that's not online. It never will be, either, most likely. It takes time to scan this stuff in."

"And time is money, yeah, yeah, yeah," Buffy said. With a sound like a thunderclap, she dropped another two volumes of bound newspapers onto the sturdy table. The librarian had provided them with a wheeled cart, but Buffy found it easier just to lug the huge tomes from point to point.

And huge they were: each with a page size slightly

larger than a modern newspaper, each five inches thick or more, and each bound with thick boards that Buffy was sure could serve as armor in a pinch. These once had been the morgue copies of the local newspaper, and of the newspapers that had preceded it. Print started dying a long time ago, really, and as the morning and afternoon dailies ceased operations, they ceded their histories and files to the papers that succeeded them, or to the library. The bound periodical collection was a treasure trove, if you thought of stuff like this as treasure.

Buffy didn't, not really. She didn't even find the papers particularly interesting. Newsprint aged badly, becoming brittle and brown and issuing a telltale acidic miasma that made her eyes sting and her nose run. She recognized the historical value of such repositories but didn't think they held any particular charm.

Willow was different, Buffy realized yet again. The other girl had a mind like a sponge, that absorbed information greedily and connected data points in ways that Buffy could only dream of. She had a lot of data to deal with too. Willow was a voracious omnivore when it came to information. Her interests were diverse and far-ranging, and she had the kind of mind that seemed equally at home soaking up info on science or mysticism, with many stops in between. Buffy knew that she herself was bright, but she knew Willow was something more than that.

Even better, Willow was an expert researcher. She'd started with generalized requests, but in the hours since they'd been there, her search had become more focused as she found and followed leads. She had brought Giles's legal pad with her and already filled more than half its remaining pages with notes of her own.

"Isn't this *fun*?" she asked.

"Yeah, loads," Buffy said. She inspected her nails. One had broken against a shelf's support bracket. "What next?"

"*Box Office Reports by Region* for 1922, 1923, and 1924," Willow said. "If they have 'em."

"Why wouldn't they?" Buffy asked. "They've got everything else down here, don't they?"

"Yup," Willow said, with an enthusiasm that bordered on outright cheerfulness. "Hollywood's been in California for a long time."

The librarian had provided them with a diagram of the lower-level stacks. Entertainment publications were on the far end of the floor, beyond the central elevator shafts and near the maintenance access tunnels. The shelving units here were particularly closely spaced, and Buffy, focused on the job at hand, hardly noticed the shadowed spaces between them.

She noticed when one of the shadows moved in her direction, though, and the blot of darkness resolved itself into something solid and real.

"Hey," Angel said. He had a book tucked under one arm.

"Hey, yourself," Buffy said, startled.

He had the most amazing way of sneaking up on a person, really, and not just in the literal sense. It was difficult sometimes for Buffy to believe that she'd known him for such a relatively short time, during which, she'd seen him only intermittently. He'd become so much a part of her life that it seemed she'd always known him.

She wondered if he felt the same.

"What brings you here?" she asked. It was daylight outside, probably late afternoon. Buffy would have liked very much to be outdoors now, away from the dust and shadow, perhaps taking an afternoon stroll. But even a brief excursion into the direct rays of the sun would reduce Angel to ash.

"Tunnels," the soft-spoken vampire said. He gestured at a nearby metal door. "Plumbing and electrical are through there, and they communicate with the storm sewers. I get around."

She nodded. "Let me put that another way," she said. "Why are you here?"

"Research," he said.

"Yes, Willow," Buffy replied, with sarcasm that was mild and gentle.

"No, really," he said. He showed her his book: *Cheap Thrills: A History of Offbeat Entertainment.* The dust jacket was a lurid illustration of a gigantic dinosaur-like beast locked in combat with an oversize gorilla.

"Don't you get enough of that kind of thing in real life?" she asked. The shelves she needed were another ten units over; she gestured for him to follow as she looked for Willow's books.

"Too much, really," Angel said.

"That doesn't look like part of the bound periodical

collection to me," Buffy said. She eyed the shelves. The library's collection of *Box Office Reports by Region* was incomplete. The volumes for 1922 and 1923 were where they were supposed to be, but then the sequence skipped ahead to 1926. Buffy shrugged and pulled the two target books, with the next one for good measure. Willow would let her know if she'd made the wrong decision.

"I was upstairs," Angel said. "I was just leaving when I heard your voices."

He didn't say anything as they walked together back to the reading room where Willow waited. For an absurd moment Buffy thought he might offer to carry her books, like a student after school, but the offer never came. That was just as well, maybe; she wasn't sure how she'd respond.

Buffy's status as the Slayer made such niceties effectively superfluous. She might lack a vampire's enhanced senses, but she was at least as strong as Angel. She was quite capable of bearing her own burdens, physically at least, and her personal preference for independent action predisposed her to do so.

Still, a girl liked to be asked.

"Hey, look who I found," Buffy said as she reentered the workroom.

Willow looked up from her notes, startled, then she grinned. "Angel!" she said. "Using the night depository?"

"Not just yet, Willow," Angel said as Buffy set the bound magazines in front of her. He looked around at the stacks of aging newspapers and magazines, and at Willow's copious notes. "What is all this?"

"Research," both girls said brightly.

"Have you heard about this sleeping sickness thing?" Buffy asked.

Angel looked at her. Very slowly, he said, "No, I haven't."

Buffy filled him in about the mysterious disorder that had struck so many of Sunnydale's youth. When she finished her summary, she added, "That's where Xander and Cordelia are now, at the hospital."

Angel nodded. "I was wondering," he said. "Buffy, this could be very serious. I've heard of things like this before. In Europe in the 1860s—"

"And in Harrisonburg, Virginia, in 1953," Willow said.

Buffy and Angel looked at her but said nothing.

Willow continued, referring to her notes, "Forty-seven students in the local college fell asleep and didn't wake up for three weeks. Ten didn't wake up at all, ever. They fell asleep and they kept sleeping."

Certain that she had their attention now, she continued. Springfield and Arlen, Pottersville and Bug Tussle, the location names were mostly obscure and picturesque, scattered across the United States and Canada. The dates she listed were similarly dispersed, following no cycle that was especially evident. One thing linked them all, though. After every paired date and location, Willow told them how many locals had fallen asleep and how many hadn't woken up.

"And something else," Willow said, concluding. "That's why I wanted the box office magazines. It looks to me like every one of these incidents happened in conjunction with a new drive-in theater, or with new management at an existing one."

"Wow," Buffy said softly. "That's quite a pattern. Why didn't anyone catch it before?"

Willow shrugged. "It's hard to see, really," she said. "They happened so far apart, and over such a long time—"

"What about here?" Buffy demanded. "What about the 'something bad' that happened years ago, that everyone keeps talking about?"

"Don't think so. There's no report of anything like this happening here, ever," Willow said. "At least not before today." She paused. "That's where we made our mistake," she said. "Sunnydale and the drive-in weren't part of the pattern, at least they weren't until now."

"So no prior 'something bad'?" Buffy asked. "Something Angel missed?"

He shot her a reproachful look.

"He didn't miss anything," Willow said. "Drive-ins are where this stuff happens. They're the context, not the cause."

"Oh." Buffy loved Willow, but there were times when she hated how the other girl talked.

"That explains it, then," Angel said. "Here."

He set his book on the table, opening it for their benefit. He pointed at a grainy photograph. "Look familiar?" he asked Buffy.

The image was eerily familiar. It was a werewolf, or a sort of werewolf. It was an unsettling fusion of man and beast, basically a human build but with animal-like head and claws. It wore a lettered varsity jacket.

"Anubis?" Willow said softly. That was the Egyptian god of the dead she'd mentioned days before, in the school library.

"No," Buffy said slowly. "But there sure is a resemblance. This is the critter Angel and I saw the other night." She looked to her vampire paramour. "You said you'd never seen anything like that before," she said, half-accusing.

"I didn't remember," Angel said.

She looked at him doubtfully. Vampires were notorious for having good memories. They could carry grudges for hundreds of years.

He explained, "I must have caught a glimpse of a movie still, or an advertisement a long time ago. Not enough to register consciously, but enough to make some kind of impression. I had to work to dredge it up."

"Wow," she said again softly, with renewed respect. To remember an experience or an enemy across the long years was impressive enough. That he could recall something barely glimpsed reminded her just how different a kind of guy she had.

"It says here that *Varsity Werewolf* was a 1958 Skull Features release," Willow said. "You guys ran into a refugee from a drive-in movie." She turned some pages, then squealed in surprise. "Hey! Look!" she said.

The book had a signature of color pages bound into its middle. One image was a sad looking girl clad in pink and white. A captioned identified her as the star of *The Lonely Cheerleader.*

"Uh-oh," Buffy said.

Willow kept turning pages. Familiar-sounding titles leaped out at them from the book, scattered though it like chocolate chips in a cookie: *Double Drunken Dragon Kung Fu Fight*, *Mysteries of Chainsaw Mansion*, *Caged Blondes*. They were the component elements of the handbill Xander had distributed so eagerly.

Willow kept skimming the pages. She paused as another still caught her eye. It was from something called *The Best Medicine*, and featured a strikingly attractive blond woman in a nurse's uniform. "Hello, Inga," she said, looking at the nurse who had ransacked Giles's holdings.

"How is this possible?" Buffy demanded, once she and Willow had explained to Angel the reason for their surprise.

"I don't know," he said, taking the book back. "Look," he said, and pointed at yet another captured image. It was of six burly gents riding motorcycles that were bigger than some cars. "Look familiar?" he asked.

She nodded. She knew what he meant. Together they'd spent a fair piece of time the night before clobbering a set of bikers who could have ridden right off this printed page.

"You said there was something like this in Europe," Willow said. Her fingertips were black with newsprint smudges. "Something like the sleeping sickness. But that was before there were movies, right?"

"Right, a long time before," Angel agreed. He paused. "But there were pup—" His words trailed off into silence.

They both looked at him expectantly.

"Well, I heard something about monks in one village fighting giant puppets," Angel said slowly. "Punch and Judy puppets."

They looked at him, united in an utter lack of understanding. Who the heck were Punch and Judy?

"Puppets?" Buffy asked.

"Punch and Judy puppets," Angel said. "Marionette shows, about a husband and wife team. All the rage, back in the day." When comprehension declined to dawn, he sighed. "I really wish Giles were here," he said. "It's a European thing."

"So do we," Buffy said. "But since he isn't—"

He took the hint. "Punch and Judy shows were blood-and-thunder stuff, entertainment for the masses. They drank and they cursed and they hit each other a lot. With clubs," he said. "And axes."

Buffy ran her fingers through her blond locks, thinking. "Sounds pretty un-PC," she said.

"Entertainment for the masses," he said again. "Cheap thrills. The shows moved from town to town."

"Giant puppets fighting monks, you say?" Buffy said.

"Life-size, anyway," Angel said. "That was the rumor, at least." He smiled, faintly and sadly. "I've been around a long time, Buffy. I hear a lot of things."

"It sounds familiar," Willow said. "I mean, marionettes are kind of like movie characters, aren't they?

And you said that there were sleeping-sickness out-breaks in the 1860s, but that was a long time after Cagliostro—"

"Cagliostro?" Angel demanded sharply, interrupting.

"That's right," Willow said. "You guys were con-temporaries. You know about him?"

"About him?" Angel repeated, with a short, sharp laugh. "I knew him. I used to go out drinking with him." He paused again. "Or, I guess you could say, Angelus did."

Buffy felt as if something cold had just run its fingers along her spine. Angelus was Angel minus the soul that gave him compassion and so much more. Angelus was the vampire Angel had been more than a century before, when he'd painted much of Europe red with fire and blood.

If this was the same Cagliostro who had been Angelus's drinking buddy back in the day, Sunnydale was in serious trouble.

"Really, ma'am, I can't suggest any specific medical or therapeutic treatment," Amanda said to the worried-looking lady on the other side of the counter. The words were a legal disclaimer, and she'd learned them by rote. The owner had been very clear on such things. The Magic Box wasn't a pharmacy or licensed health-services provider, and if Amanda ever said or did any-thing to suggest the contrary, she'd be out on her rear.

If it had been up to her, though, she'd have made her suggestions, taken the money, and let the woman have her powdered wolfsbane or dried goblin root or whatever nostrum sounded like it might do the job.

"Don't you have some kind of incense or something?" the customer asked yet again. She was plump and curly haired, a little long in the tooth for typical walk-in traffic, and her wardrobe ran to faded tie-dyes. Amanda had pretty much decided that she was some kind of over-the-hill hippie. Amanda hated hippies, but she felt a vague sympathy nonetheless. Experience with her grandparents had given her a crash course in how difficult medical challenges could be.

"You might try the Good Luck Tea," she said. "It's supposed to bring good fortune. That might help. It comes in a mint and berry blend."

She'd tried the Good Luck Tea herself. It was sour and gave her gas.

"No," the chubby lady said. "That won't work. How can I get him to drink tea when he won't wake up?"

"Huh," Amanda said. It was a reasonable question and she didn't have an answer.

"But incense, now—"

The phone rang. Amanda gestured in a mute request for patience and lifted the handset. "Thank you for calling the Magic Box," she said. Those words were rote too. "Proud provider of wondrous things to Sunnydale and surrounding environs."

"Hey," a voice said, husky and familiar. It was the heavyset guy she'd met at the teeny club earlier in the week. His name was Otto, but he preferred being called Skull.

"One moment, please," Amanda said. She covered the mouthpiece. "Incense is on the left wall, next to the candles," she told the lady with the sleepy kid. As the woman went to inspect the stock, Amanda whispered into the phone.

"I'm not supposed to take personal calls, Otto," she said, taking pains to use his real name.

"Yeah," he said. He could be a real mouth-breather. "Doing anything tonight?"

"Maybe," Amanda said slowly. Otto wasn't much, but he was more than nothing, and if she spent another night in her grandparents' house, she was going to pop like a blister. "Is there a band?"

"I was thinking movies," Otto said. "At the drive-in."

Amanda rolled her eyes. Bad enough that the townie kid had tried to pick her up, but if Otto was going to climb on the drive-in bandwagon—

Otto continued, "It's free."

"Free?" It wasn't much of a selling point, especially since Amanda had her own set of passes, but she was curious as to how Otto might have swung such a deal. She asked.

"Guy on TV," Otto said. "I saw him on the news. Belasco, or something like that."

Reflexively, Amanda corrected him. "Bal-sa-mo," she said, giving the name the rolling power that she remembered so well from the chance encounter of a few days before.

"Uh-huh," Otto said. "Really. Seemed like a nice guy. Liked him."

"He is," Amnda said. Long silence greeted her response, and she could almost hear the gears in Otto's head working, or trying to work. He was asking himself how she knew the theater owner. *She* was asking herself if she might get to see the guy again. It might be kind of nice.

"Yeah," she finally said. "I'll go to the drive-in with you, Otto."

Chapter Eleven

It was late in the day when they came for Giles. There were no windows in the washroom and he wasn't wearing a timepiece, but the air filling the enclosed space had become hot and muggy, and then had slowly cooled a bit. That meant the sun had passed its peak and was descending now. He'd been held prisoner at least half a day, maybe more.

Giles tried to use the time wisely. He ate the meal that his jailer had provided, drank plenty of water, and even performed a few exercises in an attempt to keep himself limber and aware. If any opportunity were to present itself, Giles wanted very much to be ready to take advantage. Even so, he'd become bored somewhere along the line.

That was the worst part of confinement, really: the mind-numbing monotony. A man could review the facts he held in his mind only so many times before they ran together, crying out for new information, new data, new contexts. So he was actually a bit relieved when the lock mechanism clicked and the washroom door swung back.

"Howdy, pardner," said a lean man with a wide-brimmed hat pulled low over his grizzled features. He was clad in worn black breeches and a soiled work shirt, with a Mexican serape draped across his shoulders. There was a cheroot cigar in one corner of his mouth and an antique army repeating pistol in his right hand. Another bulkier figure stood just behind him.

Giles had seen the lean man before, twice. Once when the man abducted him, and once on the television, when he'd chanced upon a western movie, vintage 1960s.

"Here's how we're goin' to do it," the gunfighter said. Curiously, the movement of his lips didn't quite match the words he spoke. "You're goin' to be a good boy, and I'm not goin' to put a hole in you. Leastways, not just yet."

"Pop him one, Pops," the gunfighter's companion said. He was a motorcyclist by the looks of him, unshaved and unwashed, and wearing a scuffed leather vest and trousers. He made a fist with his right hand and drove it into his left, to make a meaty sound that echoed in Giles's Spartan quarters. "Pop him one, and show him who's boss."

"Kids these days," the westerner said, still in a dry, whispering drawl. He stepped back a bit, and gestured for Giles to emerge. "Don't know how to treat a classy gent like you, do they?"

"No, they don't," Giles said, obeying. "But I hardly think you're the one to provide him with guidance. Why don't you introduce yourself?"

The lean man snickered. "Boss told me that you were a bug for names," he said. "I'd give you mine, but I ain't got one."

"The proverbial man with no name, eh?" Giles asked.

The response was a nod and a gestured command for him to raise his hands. Again, Giles obeyed. "Now, my friend's goin' to lead the way, but I won't be far behind. You try anythin'—you even think of trying anythin'—and you'll get a bullet in the back."

"No Spell of Entrancement this time?" Giles asked. That was most likely how they'd taken him from his home, he'd decided. He had only the vaguest of memories of that encounter, phantom images of these men and his host, wielding a lens or an amulet of some sort.

"Nope," the gunfighter agreed. "It was handy, when I came and got ya, but don't need it this time. This time there's no one local to hear."

They fell into line, the biker, then Giles, then the man with no name. Viewed from behind, the motorcyclist was remarkably simian in appearance, with stooped shoulders and a slouching gait, his head dropped low. He was silent as he led the strange trio from the improvised cell toward their destination. Giles made no move to escape as he followed the human gorilla, but he did take careful note of their surroundings.

They were about as he'd expected. The washroom was part of a building that housed a theater concession stand. A popcorn kettle, soft drink dispensers, hot dog racks, and other aluminum-clad appliances glistened. The three men walked past the appliances and outside onto a concrete walkway and then into a gravel-strewn parking area. The late afternoon sun made Giles's eyes sting and water, but he kept his hands elevated.

To his right was the curved shield of a drive-in screen. He recognized it instantly from the handbill.

"Over there, pardner," the westerner said. "On the left."

Giles turned left, keeping pace with the others as the biker led them to another structure. This one was smaller than the refreshment stand, with a low slanting roof and slit-like windows. The biker opened the door and went inside, into a smallish chamber housing projection equipment and racks that held reels of film. Giles followed, then blinked as the leather-clad ruffian passed from view.

No, not passed; vanished. He disappeared as utterly and swiftly as light did when a lamp was turned off. One moment he was there, and the next he was not.

"Very impressive," Giles said.

"I thought you would appreciate it," came the response.

Seeing his host again, Giles realized that he was correct. The man who'd brought him his fast-food luncheon had the same face as the man in his alchemy book. Differences in clothing and facial hair obscured only slightly the strong resemblance between his host and the archival image. This, indeed, was Guiseppe Balsamo, Count Cagliostro.

The motorcyclist had departed, but two other underlings remained. They scurried about the projection shack, presumably in the service of Cagliostro. One fellow wore an overcoat and a fedora, despite the heat outside. The other was the Anubis-like wolf-man Buffy had described before. Giles rather wished now that he'd given more credence to her account.

"You're something of a film aficionado, I gather," Giles said.

Cagliostro smiled. "Films are the only art form of any value that this misbegotten nation has created," he said. He pointed at his underlings and identified each in turn. "Dick Shamus, private eye," he said. "And the varsity werewolf. Behind you—"

"Is a man with no name," Giles said. "From the old American West, by way of Italy, I think."

The booth held two film projectors, each taller than a tall man. Moving in perfect coordination, the detective and the wolf-man tended to the mechanisms. Dick Shamus swung open the round door of a film-reel cover and stepped aside as the werewolf wrestled a loaded reel into place. After locking it, the detective fed a length of footage from it into the projector's inner workings and set about guiding past gears, spindles, and the bulb. Were it not for his own situation, Giles would have found the spectacle laughable. As it was, the entire sequence of events seemed more than ominous.

"Sit," Cagliostro commanded. His beard and hair

were black as night now, and the twinkle in his eyes was now a fire. Gone was the amused and indulgent aristocrat, and in his place was someone vastly less pleasant.

"I'm fine, thank you," Giles said.

The wolf-man growled, and Giles sat. The chair that Cagliostro had indicated was uncomfortable and without ornament, but sturdy. Giles knew better than to complain or resist as the gunfighter bound his wrists to the chair arms with a length of rope he took from his belt.

"And does your fondness for the cinema extend to desiring an audience?" Giles asked, honestly curious.

Cagliostro shook his head. He dropped into another chair and eyed Giles. "Not at all," he said. "But we'll open for business shortly, and it seemed wise to move you from your cell. The locals will have need of the facilities. Besides, I know all too well how unpleasant such accommodations can be to a man of learning."

"You flatter me," Giles said. "But the attention, really, is unnecessary."

Cagliostro shrugged. "I hadn't planned on finding a watcher here," he said. "I hadn't expected anything other than a sleepy California town. Really, all I'd hoped to do was visit, exhibit some motion pictures, refresh myself, and then move on. Nothing out of the ordinary, I assure you. Business as usual, I think the Americans say." He paused. "But Sunnydale has proved itself to be a most surprising place."

The words sounded odd, coming from a man with a werewolf at his beck and call.

"I discovered a curious establishment called the Magic Box," Cagliostro continued. "I had expected to find it stocked with nothing more than inexpensive novelties, and instead I found something remarkable: a matched set of Latverian soul crystals. Imagine that, Mr. Giles. A matched set! I had to destroy them, of course. Imagine how useful such a complement could be to one who knew their uses, as a weapon or a means of detection."

Giles didn't need to imagine. The owner of the Magic Box had excellent suppliers, a fine eye for value, and a remarkable attentiveness to the needs of his clientele. More than once Giles had found unexpected treasures there.

"How is it that you're in America, Count?" Giles asked bluntly. "You look remarkably well, for a dead man."

"Ah," Cagliostro said. Still seated, he tipped his head in a mocking half bow. "I'm honored that my humble story has come to the attention of the Watchers Council."

"Only obliquely," Giles said frankly. In popular literature, Cagliostro was a towering figure, legendary in stature; alchemist, occultist, and Italian nobleman, he had founded quasi-religious orders that stood the test of time, and he had performed unexplainable feats of mysticism. Supposedly, he had spearheaded the French Revolution and been plagiarized by Napoleon Bonaparte. In the annals of the Watchers, however, he was little more than a footnote, written off as a con artist and minor political schemer.

Under the circumstances, however, it seemed likely that the popular literature had the right of things.

"I came to these fair shores following the War Between the States," Cagliostro said, answering the question. "Then, as now, this was a rude nation, rough and unrefined, but it offered great promise and opportunity. It has been my home in the long years since."

"Most sources have you as deceased, circa 1795," Giles said slowly. The details were coming back to him now. "Rome tried you for heresy, magick, and conjuring and imprisoned you for life in Montefeltro."

"If it were truly for life, I would be there still, my friend," Cagliostro said. "But no. I have led many lives. I've used many names. They fall from me as the years pass, like leaves from a tree. They fall away, but I endure."

The werewolf was moving film reels from rack to rack. He dropped one, and he yelped in pain as it struck his foot. Cagliostro murmured a word that Giles couldn't quite hear, and the man-beast dissipated. Without waiting for instruction, the gunfighter picked up the dropped reel and took his fellow's place at the storage rack.

"You have no idea how pleased I am to have made your acquaintance, Mr. Giles. You seem to be an educated man, well versed in matters worth knowing," Cagliostro said. "As you can see, my current associates are less erudite. They're little more than extensions of my own will, really, and the patrons of my little enterprise are scarcely better." He paused. "I look forward to many conversations with you."

"They'll be one-sided," Giles said.

"I think not," Cagliostro said. "I have many interesting means of persuasion."

"He wasn't such a bad guy, really," Angel said. "A bit pompous. He liked to talk and he liked to drink, and he liked playing host. I don't think I paid for a single drink in the entire time I knew him. Liked to wager, too."

"This is Count Cagliostro we're talking about, right?" Willow asked. She looked skeptical. "The master alchemist played the ponies?"

The vampire nodded. They were still in the library, still in the quiet confines of the lower-level research room. Angel, however, was now at least partly in the past, wandering the labyrinth of his long and convoluted memory.

"You won't say things like that when you're older, Willow," he said. Angel was still in human mode, wearing his eternally youthful features, but his eyes looked suddenly old.

"I don't think I'll ever be as old as you," Willow said. "Um. No offense."

The vampire shook his head. "I know what you mean," he said. "But that's not what *I* mean. You'll get older. You'll see things differently. You'll see that people are more alike than they are different. They want food, drink, and companionship. Entertainment. The simple things are what make them feel human, even when they aren't."

It was the simple things that made him suffer, as well. The pleasures that most took from food and drink had been replaced by the driving need for blood, and the soul that was his curse made him an outcast among his own kind. He could enjoy existence, at least on a momentary basis, but true contentment and joy were denied to him.

"He was more than an alchemist, though. He was into many disciplines, and he was a bit of a schemer, too," Angel said. "Got drunk in a tavern one night and told me that he'd been born of common blood and spent his entire life and wits trying to rise above it. I kept telling him that all blood is pretty much the same, but he was so busy talking that he wouldn't listen."

"Wait a minute," Buffy said. "You. Knew. Cagliostro?" She paused briefly between each word, dragging out the question, clearly still having difficulty with it.

Angel knew why. In her relatively brief tenure as Slayer, she'd encountered demons and vampires by the dozen, and had somehow managed to remain in many ways a typical teenage girl, well grounded in the here and now. That was something he loved about her, one thing among many. But even though she knew full well who he was, what he was, his own apparent youth made it easier for her to look past that unpleasant truth. The comment about Cagliostro had served as a reminder.

Angel nodded. "He was a popular guy," he said. "He was sort of a doctor, too."

"A doctor?" Buffy asked, unbelieving.

"It's like the proto-science thing," Willow said. "Stuff hadn't gotten sorted out all the way just yet."

Angel nodded. "He treated Benjamin Franklin for a headache once. That was in Paris. Never let anyone hear the end of it either." Even two hundred years after the fact, he sounded annoyed. "What a blowhard."

"How dangerous is he, then?" Buffy asked. "If this is him, I mean."

"I don't know," Angel said, after a moment's thought. "The Cagliostro I knew was a charmer and a showman more than anything else. He talked a lot about transmutation and raising demons, but I never saw him do either."

"That could have been a cover," Willow said. She'd apparently finished her research and was closing the bound volumes and stacking them neatly for a return to the shelves. They made a sizeable pile. "Like in Poe's 'The Purloined Letter,' when everyone's looking for something that's been hidden in plain sight."

That made sense, Angel thought. Willow's comment cast a new light on things, making him consider them from a new perspective. Indeed, the Cagliostro of his memory had demonstrated at least one gift, even if he'd not consciously realized it at the time. He'd been an immensely likeable man, with a magnetism that defied easy description, but which could not be denied.

It wasn't easy to charm a vampire, after all.

"Is there anything else we should know?" Buffy asked.

"He was fascinated with the idea of vampirism," Angel said, remembering more and more of his late-night chats with the egotistical European. "I think that's why we got along so well. What I was—what I *am* interested him."

"He wanted to be turned?" Buffy asked. "Yecch."

Angel shook his head. "No, nothing like that. It was the metaphysical end of things that he liked. He wanted to run tests and do experiments," he said. Again he smiled. "But I knew better than that."

"Oh," Buffy said.

"We lost touch after the French Revolution, of course," Angel said.

"Of course," Willow said.

"That's about it," Angel said, returning to the present again. "But you believe he's running the drive-in?"

"Well, that's what Xander was telling us," Buffy said. "You didn't see anything suspicious out there?"

"Nothing," he said. "Just a nervous security guard. But, Buffy, the place wasn't open for business yet."

Buffy sighed. Xander wasn't there to see it, but he got his wish. "I guess we're going to the movies, then," she said.

Chapter Twelve

The phone on the nightstand buzzed. The sound wasn't loud, but it was enough to rouse Xander from his light, uncomfortable sleep. He blinked in surprise as vague dreams fled his conscious mind, leaving behind phantom images of reporting for a biology final while clad only in his gym shorts. He rubbed his eyes, momentarily disoriented, and then reality reasserted itself. He was still in the white-finished hospital room, and nothing seemed to have changed much since his last waking moment. Jonathan remained still beneath the bed sheets, his eyes moving beneath their lids. The bedside monitor continued its work, and the air was thick with that wonderful hospital scent, the smell of sick people and medicine.

The phone buzzed again. He stood and went to answer it. The catnap had helped, but he was still tired, and a bit stiff from sitting in the chair for however long it had been. He had a bad taste in his mouth and his lips were dry; he licked them before answering.

"Xander?" Buffy's familiar voice asked.

"Yeah," he answered. There was a pitcher of water on the nightstand and a pair of drinking glasses. He eyed them thirstily. "What's up, Buff?

"You're still there?" she asked. "Your mom said she didn't know where you were, but I thought you'd have gone home by now."

How late was it? He looked for a clock but didn't see one. From the looks of the sky outside, however, visible through the room's window, it was very late afternoon at the earliest. The sky had begun to darken, just a bit.

"What time is it?" he asked. Then, after she told him, he whistled softly. He'd been asleep for hours. He must have been more fatigued than he'd thought. Jonathan's still-slumbering form was a reminder that another explanation might apply, but Xander chose to hold on to the mundane. He'd been up all night, after all.

"Sorry," he said. "Yeah, I'm still here. What's up?"

As Buffy told him what she and Willow had learned, and about Angel's contribution, Xander drank some water. It was rude, he knew, but he couldn't help himself. Buffy's account was rapid and precise, but curiously uninvolving. Usually he found these things fascinating, but not now. Maybe it was because he was hearing them in the worrisome context of the hospital room, but her words simply didn't draw him in.

"That's great, Buff," he said, trying hard to be sincere. "I mean, not great, but—"

"I know what you mean," she said.

"Do you want me to come with?" he asked. Even to him the offer sounded unenthusiastic. Maybe it was that famed Buffy focus on all things Slayerish, but she hadn't asked how he was, or if there'd been any change in Jonathan's situation. She hadn't even asked if he had spoken to any of the doctors. Ordinarily, such oversights were business as usual and perfectly understandable, but right now, in the last of his sleep hangover, the oversight rankled slightly.

She must have heard it in his voice. Even over the phone her sigh was audible. "You're worried about them, aren't you?" she asked, more gently now. "All of them, I mean."

"Yeah." There wasn't much more to say.

"Look, Xander, we know that this character can send minions out, to do his work. Maybe you'd better stay there, keep an eye out," she said. "You know?"

"Yeah," he said again, but this time more gratefully. Deliberately or not, she'd said just the thing he needed to hear. Now he could stay without feeling guilty.

"Is Cordy there?" Buffy asked.

"I haven't seen her." The idea that the Queen of Sunnydale High would spend her Saturday afternoon in a hospital visiting sick friends seemed unlikely. Cordelia had shown surprising depths to Xander in some of their private moments, but he didn't think she'd come that far, not just yet.

"Her Dad says she went out," Buffy said.

Xander felt a pang of worry. "It's early for the Bronze," he said.

"He said she went out hours ago," Buffy replied. A moment's silence stretched between them before she continued. "I'm sure she's fine, Xander. Cordy can take care of herself. But I'll keep an eye out."

He told her he'd do the same, and then, at her prompting, told her as much as he could about the drive-in itself. Before being banished to handbill duty, Xander had undertaken many chores on the site, most of them somewhat demeaning. According to Buffy, Angel had taken a quick look-see too, but Xander knew the place better. He was able to provide reasonable details about what went where, who to go to, and what to see.

"Good," she said. "That'll help." She paused. "Xander, this really isn't your fault, you know."

Jonathan's beside monitor chirped again, another reminder. Xander eyed it and then his sleeping classmate. Jonathan seemed unchanged, but Xander couldn't be certain. Sometimes staring at something too long blinded you to its details.

"Isn't it?" he said, not quite bitterly.

"No, it's not," Buffy said. Now her words were nearly a command. "Look, think about it. We know something like this has been going on for at least two hundred years. Jonathan was just in the wrong place at the wrong time."

"Emphasis on *wrong*," Xander said. "And because I put him there."

"Yeah, like you put Aura there?" Buffy said.

"But Aura wasn't—Oh," Xander said, realizing what she meant. "The others were," he said.

"Not all of them," Buffy told him. "Look, we can talk about this later, but there's no reason to tear yourself up. You didn't do anything wrong and you're helping now."

"Yeah," Xander said. "Helping."

"Take care of yourself, Xander," Buffy said. "That way, you can take care of the rest of us."

She ended the conversation on that oddly philosophical note. Xander shrugged and replaced the handset. He glanced at Jonathan, then at the monitor, and then out the window at the darkening sky.

There wasn't much else to do, really.

"Am I getting old?" Buffy asked, hanging up the phone.

"Huh?" Willow asked. She could not have looked more confused had Buffy sprouted a second head. The question threw her for a loop.

"Don't be silly," Angel chimed in. "You're just growing up. That was pretty mature advice you gave him at the end there."

"No, it's not that," Buffy said. She sounded half-amused, half-confused. "It's just, Xander doesn't want to go to the drive-in with me. I must be losing my girl-ish good looks."

They were in her room at the Summers house. Joyce was nowhere in sight, and the note she'd left just said that she'd gone out with a friend. That was just as well. Buffy had preparations to make and didn't want to have to provide excuses for Angel's presence in her room.

Some of those preparations were prosaic enough: a quick shower and a change into something stylish but durable, since there was almost certain to be some violence in the offing. That violence was also why she and the others were taking quick inventory of her personal arsenal, choosing what was likely to come in handy.

"These things Cagliostro has are bad news," she told Willow. "And they don't hold to the usual rules, to judge from that wolf-guy. I'm guessing that the traditional crosses and such won't be much use."

"If they're made out of ectoplasm, you're probably right," Willow said. She set the crosses and holy water aside to make space for more pragmatic tools, being careful not to wave the blessed items in Angel's direction. Rules were rules, after all, and Angel very definitely was a vampire, no matter how good a guy he was. "It's funny," she continued. "Alchemy's bound up in the kabbalah."

"Kabbalah?"

"Ancient Jewish sorcery," Willow said. "I wish I knew more about it. Maybe I could help with some kind of hoodoo—"

"I don't think that's a good idea, Willow," Angel said. "Magicks are bad news, unless you know what you're doing, and dabbling in a new discipline is especially bad. Besides, old Guissepe may be an alchemist, but that doesn't mean this is alchemy proper that we're talking about."

Buffy knew what he meant. They'd talked about it

on the way home from the library. This was more of the hide-in-plain-sight stuff; Angel had suggested that, even back in the day, Cagliostro might have used expertise in one field to divert attention from others. Everything she'd heard so far suggested that he had pursued many lines of inquiry into the workings of the universe, and this was no time to try to second-guess him. It was better to stick with what she knew worked.

That meant knives. Knives and axes and swords, and other edged things that could slice pieces off the conjurer's cat's-paw agents. A dozen deadly implements lay arrayed on Buffy's chenille bedspread, incongruous-looking on the frilly thing. "Take your pick," she told the others.

Angel went for the largest implement of death, of course. He was a guy, after all, even if an undead one. He picked a Roman-style short sword, thick and solid but honed to a razor edge. The air whistled as he test-swung it, and he nodded in approval. "I'm ready," he said.

"This one's pretty," Willow said. She selected a wavy-bladed dagger with a red stone set in its hilt, and banded decorations that bore cryptic runes.

"You're sure about this, Willow?" Buffy asked. She wasn't. Xander, by his absence, had reminded her yet again that taking civilians into battle wasn't always the best strategy. Willow was smart and brave, but there were things in life that simply weren't meant for nonslayers.

"Hey! You're not leaving me behind," Willow said. She was very pretty, in an impish sort of way, but also very good at showing irritation. "I've been through a lot lately, you know."

"Okay," Buffy said, resigned. This was an argument she never seemed to win. "In that case, ditch the pretty knife. Take this instead."

She handed Willow a battle-axe, like the one she'd used the night before, but smaller and lighter; Willow didn't have a slayer's strength, after all. "Chop with it," she said. "Stabbing holes in these things doesn't do much good, but cutting pieces off does."

"So it's an issue of structural integrity, hey?" Willow said. She hefted the weapon and tried to make a snarl, but she was just too cute to make the effect work.

"Just hang back and follow our lead," Buffy told her. "Let Angel and me handle the heavy lifting. Don't be afraid to run if we tell you to."

Willow nodded.

Coins rattled in the machine's inner workings, and numbers lit next to the slot. She fed it two dollars in quarters, which was all she could find in the depths of her handbag. As she considered her snack choices, Cordelia wondered when the modern world would make its way to Sunnydale. If this thing were able to read credit cards, like they could in civilized places, she'd be able to buy it out.

After a bit of mix-and-match, she settled on Twizzlers and a bag of those baked potato chip things, the former for their durability and the latter out of consideration for her figure. Either had to be much better than the cafeteria's grim fare, which ran to salted fat. At least they were prepared by national manufacturers. She stooped to claim her purchases from the machine's chute.

"You *are* here," Xander said.

She whirled, startled. He stood behind her, framed in the doorway of the alcove that held the snack machines.

"I thought I saw you walk by," he continued. He looked bad—not bad ugly, but bad tired and bad worried.

"Huh? What? Yeah," Cordelia said.

"How long?" he asked.

"A while," she said. The next words didn't come as easily as she would have liked them to. "I was worried about Aura," she said. "I didn't want her to be alone."

"Yeah, I know," Xander said sympathetically. "But everyone's doing what they can, and the doctors say there's nothing anyone can do. Jonathan's signs are all good, except for this pesky sleep thing."

Cordelia tried to muster some sympathy for Xander's little friend, but with only the slightest success. She had other things on her mind.

"Aura's been here for days, Xander," she said. "She was the first, and they say she's getting weaker."

"I don't think they're telling us everything, Cordy," Xander said seriously. "In fact, I know they aren't. I heard the doctors talking. The longer this thing lasts, the less likely it is that they'll wake up." He paused. "Wake up ever, I mean."

"Why would they hide something like that?" she asked.

He shrugged. "Worried about a panic, I guess," he said. He sounded worried.

Without asking, he fell in beside her as she left the vending-machine room. The hospital was only lightly staffed, for whatever reason, and no one seemed to take note of them as they paced down the corridor toward the patient rooms.

"Buffy called," Xander said. "She asked after you."

"How sweet," Cordelia said, without particular sincerity. "Any news on the Giles front?"

"Yeah, Willow thinks she's figured it out," Xander said. "Whoops. Here's my stop."

Cordelia followed him into Jonathan's room. Remarkably, the place had an unoccupied bed. Again without any conscious coordination, they sat on it, side by side, but with a reasonable distance between them.

Even so, Cordy had a feeling about where things were headed.

"Twizzler?" she asked, only to have him decline. That was a surprise. Xander nearly never turned down food, and the ropy candy strands qualified as food, at least on a technicality.

Rather than accept the proffered sugary treat, he gave her a quick rundown on what Buffy had told him about Willow's research and about their plans for a run to the open-air theater. It was a lot to take in, but Cordelia managed.

"Well, to be honest, that sounds pretty logical to me," she said. "I'm not sure about Willow, but Buffy and Angel are the right choice for that kind of thing." Buffy and Angel had enhanced capabilities, and each could do things that Cordelia even now found amazing.

"Yeah," Xander said. "It's just—I feel so helpless."

"I know," Cordelia said. She'd never seen him like this before. Xander could be irritating and a bit of a buffoon, but he never seemed to lack self-confidence. Clearly, he had hidden depths.

"What about you?" he asked.

"Nothing better to do," she lied, biting into her cherry red candy.

They sat together in effective silence for another minute or two, Cordelia eating and Xander watching her eat. The air seemed thick with apprehension, apprehension concerning their friends who were in the hospital and those who weren't.

Then something remarkable happened. Xander managed a smile. "Cordy," he said, "I changed my mind. I think I will have some of that."

He kissed her, hard, and she kissed him back. He pulled her to him and she pulled too, until they fell back on the bed in a mutual embrace.

What the heck. It beat necking in a broom closet.

Traffic was bad; everyone in town seemed to have picked tonight to go to the movies. The road that led out of Sunnydale was heavily trafficked with cars and vans, pickup trucks and SUVs. The procession looked like it included a pretty good sampling of town society, and Buffy had a bad feeling about that. Even now, even with the sun beneath the horizon, the caravan continued. Parking would be at a premium tonight.

"This is going to take forever," Angel said. He was seated behind the steering wheel of Giles's little car, which they had commandeered for the evening. Buffy had called shotgun, leaving the backseat for Willow.

"Do the best you can," the Slayer said. Eyeing the seeming endless procession that stretched before them, she worried that even Angel's best wouldn't be good enough.

"Everyone buckled up?" he asked.

"I am," Willow said.

"Buffy?"

"Oh, all right," she said, and pulled the woven belt into place and clicked the buckle shut.

He grinned wolfishly at her. "Thanks," he said.

"Don't you think you're being a little—*Yow!*"

The next twenty minutes or so were as frightening as any in Buffy's young life. Angel drove the little car with unrelenting aggression and the skill of someone who could combine superhuman reflexes with lessons learned through decades of experience. Immediately they were darting in and out among the other vehicles. The compact's engine coughed and stuttered but never failed as Angel called on all of its strength. He snapped the wheel from side to side, exploiting every opportunity to gain even a few car lengths' distance. He swerved on and off the road, spraying gravel as he used the roadbed shoulder to pass illegally on the right. By the time they'd arrived at the drive-in, and Angel had forced his way into the front of the line, Buffy was very nearly carsick.

The ticket seller was an older man, balding and

portly and dressed in black. "It's free tonight," he said affably. "But we're running out of spaces." He leaned down from the booth opening, as if to say something more. As he did, Buffy realized something odd: He was wearing a priest's collar.

That should have been her first clue.

"Hey," the man said, "aren't you Angelus?"

"Huh?" Angel said, more perplexed than alarmed by the use of his old name.

"DIE, VAMPIRE!" the ticket-selling priest screamed, stabbing at him with a wooden stake.

Chapter Thirteen

"I see that we have visitors," Cagliostro said, in tones that were free of his earlier bombast. He sounded eerily calm, even detached, and his voice seemed to come from a distance. "The Slayer and her pet vampire. You really must explain that situation to me, when we have the time."

"If you survive," Giles said. He tested his bonds again, but they remained secure.

Cagliostro didn't seem to notice his actions or his words. Still facing Giles from his own chair near the big projectors, he seemed absolutely unconcerned with any challenge that Giles might offer. His gaze was trained in Giles's direction but seemed focused on something else entirely. The effect was disconcerting. It was as if he were looking not *at* the Watcher but *through* him. The confines of the projection booth were filled by the clatter of the running projector, but his placid tones cut through the noise with remarkable clarity. They were nearly alone in the place; only the nameless gunfighter shared it with them as he tended the equipment.

"You'll talk to me later, Rupert," Cagliostro said. His lips twitched as he used Giles's first name for the first time, but the hint of a smile faded almost instantly. "There's much you'll have to explain to me, once I've taken my leave of this remarkable settlement. I've long been curious about the inner workings of the Council."

Giles said nothing. There was no point. He'd never permit Cagliostro—never permit anyone—to extract such knowledge from him, but displays of defiance would do him no good. Better to allow events to play out and wait for an opportunity.

"This land must offer great frustrations to a man with a watcher's education," Cagliostro said dreamily. "So much ignorance—"

"So much vigor," Giles said in correction. He certainly had issues with the so-called New World—what Americans did to food bordered on the barbarous—but the bonds he'd made here were strong and ran deep. There was no point in countenancing insults.

"Ignorant cattle," Cagliostro said, still speaking with a distracted air. "Peasants who don't know that they are peasants. Like sheep without a shepherd."

That was the second time he'd used animals as a metaphor. Were they simply the first insults that came to mind, or had the alchemist inadvertently revealed something of himself? Did he think of people as a means of sustenance? That thought, coupled with his host's longevity, hinted at an unpleasant possibility.

"There's something of the vampire in you, isn't there?" Giles asked.

Cagliostro actually laughed at that. "Quite the contrary," he said. "Rather there is something of me in at least some vam — *Uh!*"

He flinched. As Giles watched, fascinated, Cagliostro slumped slightly. The smooth composure of his features broke again, and an expression of pain flickered across his face, almost too quickly to be seen. He bit his lower lip and murmured, "Well struck, Slayer. First blood."

He was speaking of Buffy, Giles realized — perhaps even *to* her.

How could that be?

Angel was fast but not quite fast enough. He gave a gasp of pain as the stake penetrated his chest. His evasive maneuver hadn't failed completely, though; the spear of wood stabbed into him just below the collarbone and into the joint of his shoulder. It missed his heart entirely.

Buffy's speed served them both even better. She drew the *boka* and swung it in a short arc that passed through the priestly ticket seller's wrist. The hand that had held the stake separated instantly, and the remainder of their adversary vanished nearly as fast.

"Th-thanks," Angel said. He pulled the wooden stake from his shoulder with a wet tearing noise. "Took me by surprise."

"You okay?" Buffy asked.

"I'll live," Angel said. He moved his injured joint tentatively. "Hurts," he said. "Hurts, but it works."

"End of the line. Everyone out," Buffy snapped, kicking open her door. "Now!"

"We can't just leave the car—," Willow started to say.

"Now!" Buffy said. Her earlier misgivings about Willow's presence belatedly reasserted themselves, but what was done, was done. The here and now were what mattered.

Horns honked as they scrambled from the car, and other drivers shouted, making their displeasure known. The line behind them was long, and couldn't move now, with the path blocked. That was to the good, Buffy decided. According to Angel and Xander both, this was the establishment's only entryway. That meant there'd be fewer bystanders to worry about.

Not that there weren't plenty, she thought as she viewed the entirety of the drive-in for the first time. With the parking area lit by the screen's reflected radiance, Buffy could see the place was nearly full. There were scores of vehicles—perhaps hundreds. No one went to the movies alone; if there were even two people in each car . . .

"We've got to get moving," she said. She pointed to a distant building, squat and low. A beam of light spilled from one window. "There. I'm thinking, the projection booth. If we're talking magick movies, that's where we need to be."

She took the lead, in part because of her own anxiety and in part to give Angel a moment to recover.

Moving quickly, they followed her along an improvised path that snaked between parked cars. *Boka* in one hand, a simple machete in the other, she did her best to use the terrain to her advantage, darting between parked cars to block prying eyes, however briefly.

The priest's greeting still rang in her ears. For the vampire it had been a threat; to her it had meant something else, or two somethings.

They'd come to the right place. If ever she'd doubted that, she was certain now.

And Cagliostro was ready for them.

"Coffee?" Barney asked. He offered his thermos, and when Joyce nodded, he topped off her cup.

Now that they'd arrived at the open-air theater, Joyce felt a little silly for having accepted his invitation. These were hardly the kind of movies for a grown woman to watch. Her tastes ran more to love stories and art films, but she couldn't image them running in a place like this.

And if she felt silly, it wasn't a bad feeling. Being silly reminded her of being young. There was an electric excitement in the air that helped her momentarily forget that she was a middle-aged woman out on a lark with a man who was more of a friendly acquaintance than anything else.

"I remember this one," Barney said as the image of a grizzled, world-weary man in western garb filled the screen."

Joyce did too. She'd seen *Reach for the Sky*—and

Die! with Buffy's father on its first run, in a conventional theater, back when the world was younger. She'd been younger too, of course, but her memory wasn't gone yet. She reviewed the handbill. Black letters on orange were hard to read in the reflected light, but she managed. "It's not on the list," she said, puzzled.

"Coming attractions," Barney said, staring raptly at the screen's display. "Man, this was so—Hey!"

The gunfighter was gone. In a convulsive wrench, its image had given way to something else. Cheap-sounding music, made up mostly of chimes and woodwinds, spilled from the car speakers, and the title frame of a movie appeared on the screen. It was for some kind of martial arts film, Joyce realized, annoyed. Movies ran on twinned projectors, she knew, switching off between them as films ended. Someone had botched the changeover and transitioned from the previews to the main program.

"We can rent it sometime, if you want," she told Barney, trying to console him. "The western, I mean. It might be fun to see at home."

"Well struck, Slayer. First blood," Cagliostro said.

Even as Cagliostro's brief expression of discomfort faded, the gunfighter moved to act, as Giles watched carefully. One leathery hand grasped a lever extending from the first projector, and one booted foot came down on a pedal connected to the other. Hand and foot acted simultaneously, and the pitch of projector motors abruptly shifted. One unit was shutting down, Giles realized, and the other was coming to life.

Something else was happening too.

It wasn't natural light but a different kind of light that was emerging from the second lens. It didn't follow a conventional radiance's straight path, but it looped and curled. Like a serpent's tongue or a demon's tentacle, it writhed and undulated as it extended itself into the open area between Giles and Cagliostro. One end remained securely anchored to the projector lens, while the other did a delicate dance in the electricity-charged air, as if on a quest. Once, the latter end came ominously close to Giles's eyes, and Cagliostro chucked softly.

"How odd. The lens likes you," he said. His tone was still distant and cool, as if he spoke from the depths of a dream. "It doesn't like everyone. But it likes me more."

As if drawn by the tranquil voice, the glowing tendril shifted in midair. It had moved slowly before, but now, almost too swiftly for the eye to follow, it darted in Cagliostro's direction. It darted, struck, and buried itself in his chest. The alchemist gave another gasp, a sound that could have been pleasure or pain. Almost instantly the tendril began to pulse and throb.

"There. That's much better," the gunfighter said.

He spoke with Cagliostro's voice.

Buffy was leading the others past one real behemoth of an SUV when the wolf-man dropped on her from above. She felt rather than saw or heard his presence, spinning just in time to see his dark form against the darker sky.

"You again," she said, and swung her machete. The wolf-man's head went flying with gratifying speed, and his body disappeared, dissipating into the night air. Willow gave a squeal of surprise, and Buffy realized that she'd never seen the effect. She glanced in her friend's direction and said, "See? Like a light turning off."

"Buffy, look out!" Angel shouted.

It was happening again: same SUV, same varsity werewolf, like instant replay or a summer rerun. Buffy chopped at the doppelganger quickly, but not fast enough. He had taken her unawares. Her slash went off-course and the beast hit her. The impact sent her tumbling to the ground, with the monster crouched on top of her. She raised both weapons to defend herself, but like an expert wrestler the wolf-man's clawing hands clamped down on her wrists, blocking both of her strikes. Forcing her arms apart to give himself easier access, the creature lowered his jaws to her throat.

"Mmmm," Cordelia said, then broke the kiss and came up for air. "You've got your failings, mister, but you're a good kisser."

"Yeah?" Xander said. He swallowed the last of the candy. "What's that thing in English grammar?" he asked. "Nominative, comparative—"

"Huh?" Cordelia asked. The nonsequitur made no sense.

"I don't want to be good," Xander said, but it wasn't a complaint. He said with a smile, "I don't want to be better, either. Let me show you that I'm the best."

He locked lips with her again, and pulled her even closer. They were still rolling around on the unassigned bed, but Cordelia didn't intend to let things go any further.

Some small corner of her mind was still filled with surprise with herself for the unscheduled make-out session. This was different from the other times, somehow richer and more textured. She knew that there was still danger afoot, but there was something more. There was Jonathan and there was Aura, and the mysterious malady they shared. The mysterious illness was what her English teacher termed "an intimation of mortality"—a reminder of how fleeting life could be, and Cordelia enjoyed life very much.

Xander was coming in for another pass when something caught Cordelia's eye. Over his shoulder she could see something moving.

"Ooomp!" she said, pushing him back.

"Ooomp?" he asked, baffled.

"L-look," she said, pointing. "Look at Jonathan!"

That did it. He gave up trying and turned to look at his slumbering classmate. Jonathan was still asleep, still . . . still. He lay unmoving, as if frozen in time, but something was different.

A glowing line of something had drifted in through the window. It traced a lazy, meandering track to Jonathan's chest and attached itself to him directly above the heart. In the room's bright lights it was difficult to see clearly, but as Cordelia and Xander watched, that changed. The line thickened and resolved itself, until it looked solid and real. Then it began to pulse, with a rhythm that Cordelia found unnervingly familiar.

It was like the beating of a human heart.

Buffy felt the beast's hot breath on the skin of her neck and tried to push him back and up to free herself. The effort was futile. He had leverage and she didn't. The wolf-man's bared fangs came closer and closer. Saliva dripped onto her face, hot and disgusting.

There was a sound of impact. Something solid slammed into the wolf-man from behind. The varsity werewolf instantly blurred and faded, and then the thing was gone.

"Take that, foul beast of darkness," Willow said. She still held the edged weapon and seemed remarkably pleased with herself. Buffy didn't blame her; it had been a good strike. Willow would have made a fine avenging fury, if avenging furies came in a Jewish pixie variety.

Buffy glanced at Angel. He opened his hands and shrugged, as if to excuse himself for not coming to her aid first. "I'm faster, but she was closer," he said.

"Yeah, yeah, yeah," Buffy said, catching her breath and leading them forward. "I—for gosh sakes. Will you look at that?"

They'd rounded the SUV's sheltering bulk now and could see the bowl-like parking area of the drive-in. The view was much like what they had seen before, with an awe-inducing difference. The cars and trucks and vans remained where they were, but now lines of pale fire emerged from half of them. Narrow and faint, the tracks the lines followed were fluid and undulating, like vines blowing in the wind.

"Wow," Willow said.

"Yeah, wow," Buffy said, struck by the mysterious tableau. It was strangely beautiful. The silvery tendrils branched and converged, bent and doubled and looped. In school, Buffy had seen documentary footage shot underwater, films of jellyfish trailing tendrils in sub-sea splendor. What she saw now reminded her of those films. Each had one thing in common: one end led to a parked vehicle and the other led to the projection shack.

"What is it?" Willow asked. Buffy could tell that her friend was desperately trying to make sense of it. "It looks—it looks like some kind of fiber-optic network."

"No," Angel said. "Those are silver cords," he said.

"Huh?"

"I told you, Cagliostro was a dabbler. He followed a lot of belief systems," Angel said. "He told me once about spiritualism, and about out-of-body experiences." He paused. "The silver cord is what ties the spirit to the body. He pulled their souls to him. He's feeding from them."

Chapter Fourteen

"It's easier here," Cagliostro said. "I imagine I have your Hellmouth to thank for that. I can do more than I could ever do before."

He was still speaking through the gunslinger, but his voice had a curious echoing quality now. It was somewhat like hearing a stereo broadcast with the channels out of phase, and the effect varied as the gunslinger paced back and forth.

"It's hardly *my* Hellmouth," Giles said. He knew the meaning behind the alchemist's words, though. Sunnydale sat atop the Hellmouth, a portal that led to nearly every imaginable evil. Most texts characterized the Hellmouth as a mere gateway, but that was simply a concrete image intended to make things more easily understood. Certainly, the Hellmouth was a hole that led to various hells and such, but it was a cauldron, too, seething with endless dark power. He knew that the drive-in was outside the town limits, but it perched at the very rim of the Hellmouth. Here, now, with someone like Cagliostro in command, surely enough stray energies drifted up from its depths to make a difference.

"You can't imagine how it feels," Cagliostro said. The gunfighter's body paced steadily, as if to expend nervous energies. "I can do so much more now. I'm in so many different places, so many different forms—"

The gunfighter's outlines shifted. He became shorter, squatter. His serape lengthened into an overcoat and his hat restyled itself. "See what I mean?" he asked. "I developed the ability to field agents like this centuries ago, and to direct them to act on my behalf. But it's only since coming here that I could extend myself into them, and exercise my other abilities through them." He was Dick Shamus now.

Yet again Giles tested his bonds, in the vain hope that the rope might have vanished along with the gunslinger who had brought it. No luck. The ropes indeed were gone, but steel handcuffs had taken their place. Even Cagliostro's props had made the transition from one identity to the next. "You really do like the movies," Giles continued.

Dick Shamus nodded. "The images, the color, the verve—vastly more impressive than mere puppetry. Mr. Edison was quite a fellow. I had dinner with him once, you know."

"I hadn't," Giles said drily.

"I was in the magick lantern business then," Cagliostro mused. "Stage shows, with projected images. A transitional form. Better than puppet shows, too. It served my purposes well enough."

"And before that?"

Dick Shamus reverted to the gunslinger. "Minstrel shows. Before that, puppet shows. Punch and Judy, and that rot. Any mass entertainment that draws crowds," he said. "Anything that brings the cattle to me, so that I may connect with them. They come, I drain their spirit-force, and I add it to my own. In olden times, I had to do it directly, but now, here—"

"You have these—these proxies," Giles prompted.

Cagliostro nodded. "Extensions of myself, made from the stuff of souls. Mere puppets anywhere else, but here, they are extensions of myself," he said again. "I can use them to—"

"Prey on anyone unfortunate enough to make their acquaintance," Giles said.

"*Harvest* is a more appropriate word, I think," Caligostro said. "And not *anyone*. It varies by popula-tion. I've found more here who are susceptible to the charm than anywhere else. I don't know why, really. It must be the Hellmouth, either strengthening me or weakening them. The numbers rise by the minute." He paused. "Isn't it odd? I'd sent the wolf and the others out merely to get the lay of the land, and instead, they've fed me."

"You're a monster," Giles said.

The gunfighter laughed, a stereo chuckle that was deep and complex. When he spoke, the seated Cagliostro's lips moved too, and words emerged from both mouths. "I'm but a dabbler and an explorer," he said. "In all my journeys I've never pretended to be more. But I think that when the time comes to leave this pleasant community, I may well be something more." Two heads tilted, and four eyes gazed at Giles. "I might be something like a god."

Booted feet gritted on gravel. The sound made Buffy turn just in time to see someone or something emerge from the darkness between two parked panel vans. She saw a figure in black leather with skin that was as white as bone and hair that showed as purple even in the poor light. Reflexively, the Slayer raised her machete and swung.

"Hey!" The voice was girlish and angry. Cardboard containers of popcorn and soda flew, scattering their contents as Buffy's target tired to dodge.

It was a civilian on her way back from the concession stand. Just in time, Buffy pulled back and changed the path of her blade. There was a tearing thump as the machete slammed into one of the panel vans, embedding itself deeply in the metal.

"What is your problem, witch?" the Goth girl asked. She made a great show of brushing popcorn from the front of her outfit. "You made me drop my stuff!"

"Sorry," Buffy said. An apology certainly seemed in order, but her heart wasn't in it.

"Otto is going to kill me!" the girl said.

Heaven might know who Otto was, but Buffy didn't. "Really, I'm sorry," she said.

"You're going to pay for that," the Goth girl said, but then her mouth opened in a silent O of surprise.

She'd seen Buffy's machete and *boka,* and realized the Slayer's companions carried weapons too. "Hey," she said, turning even paler, "I don't want any trouble."

"You won't get any," Buffy said, brushing past her. Calling back over her shoulder she said, "And get out of here if you can. Walk out if the entrance is still blocked."

She'd just finished speaking when the next wave of attack came.

Xander was being stupid again, Cordelia realized as she reentered the hospital room. She was out of breath from her hasty patrol of the corridor, but she managed to draw enough air into her lungs to shape the words. "Get away from that!" she commanded.

He tore his gaze from the thread of light. It was much thicker now and flared where it met Jonathan's chest. Xander's fingertips were inches from the gleaming line.

"Huh?" he asked, startled. The sudden movement almost brought him into contact with the tendril, and Cordelia gasped in concern. "Okay, okay," he said, drawing back. "It's just—it doesn't look like much."

"Neither do the others," Cordelia said. She was relieved, but she still watched carefully in case Xander did something that was, well, Xander-like.

"Others?"

She nodded. "I checked every room I could find without getting caught. Everyone I could find who's like—like him, has one of those things coming out of their chests," she told him.

According to news reports, the hospital held thirty victims of the mysterious sleeping sickness. Cordelia had found only half that number, but they had all been much alike. Friends or strangers, teenage or adult, they all lay unmoving beneath white sheets, with silvery luminances sprouting from their chests like some strange plant.

Worst of all was Aura. The sight of her had nearly made Cordelia weep. Her friend's skin had paled further, and the heart monitor's panel suggested that she was at the lower margin of safety. She'd thumbed the call button but left Aura's room before anyone had arrived.

"All of them, huh?" Xander said. He leaned closer to the strand and eyed it suspiciously. "It doesn't look like much."

"Maybe not one, but I assure you, seeing more than a dozen of those things will give you the creeps," Cordelia said.

"Huh." Xander was repeating himself. "I wonder what it is?"

"So do I," Cordy said. "And once Buffy gets back from the drive-in, I'm sure that she and Giles will tell us all about it."

"I wonder how it connects up?" Xander asked, speaking more to himself than to her. He brought his fingers close to it again. "I bet I could tear it loose."

"Xander!" She nearly screamed his name, but she was too late.

He'd already touched it.

• • •

After a certain point the process became monotonous. Dodge, hack, then dodge or strike again. There were nights when slaying had a certain rhythm to it, like an elaborate dance of strike and counterstrike, but not tonight. This was extermination, pure and simple.

Another wolf-man leaped at her, so she swung one blade to remove his head and the threat. Hollywood's idea of a vampire—presumably from the same movie that had given form to the ticket-selling priest—lunged with fangs bared, then died as she lopped off an arm with a lucky swing. In real life, that wouldn't have worked, but Buffy didn't have time to be thankful for her relative good fortune. Inga was coming at her with a chainsaw and needed to be put down. Buffy dispatched her, only to have to do it again as another kill-crazy Swedish nurse materialized out of nowhere.

"How're you holding up, Buffy?" Angel called out to her. He was busily decapitating a biker brute but whirled just in time to fend off another priest and then a cheerleader.

"Could be better," she said, panting. "Could be worse."

She was serious. The sheer number of assailants was daunting, but they were vulnerable individually. Now that they knew how to destroy the phantasms, it was just a matter of being wary and strong. Even Willow was keeping pace, thanks in part to protective cover from Slayer and vampire. For whatever reason, the movie afterimages were concentrating on vampire and Slayer, and not on their little friend. They were making progress. It was slow, hard work, but the distance between them and their goal dwindled gradually.

Allowing Willow to come along had been a mistake, though. More and more, Buffy was sure of that. The farther they went, the greater the resistance became, and that worried Buffy. Sooner or later, she could be worn down. So could Angel. If either of them was struck down, the balance would tip from their favor and all would fall. They had to reach Cagliostro before that happened.

Three bikers attacked, whipping chains. Buffy sliced at them, first the chains and then the goons who wielded them. As she swung and spun, Angel extinguished a kung fu fighter in midkick. He was in full vampire mode now, and the grin he flashed at her was both bestial and reassuring.

It was good to have a boyfriend who appreciated your profession.

The projection shack neared. The attacks came more furiously, increasing in number and intensity. Buffy swung and cut and swung some more, then called out, "Willow!"

"Yeah?" came the answer. Willow took another slice at some guy wearing an overcoat and a slouch hat.

"This is where you get off," Buffy said.

"No!'

"Yes!" she made it a command. They were mere yards from the doorway now, and Buffy could no longer spare her friend the protective attention she needed. "Break and take cover. I mean it!"

"I won't leave you!" Willow said, but her voice

was failing. She was wearing down. It was amazing
that she'd made it this far, really.

"Now!" Buffy repeated. "It's time for the profes-
sionals to take over."

Xander felt as if he'd gripped a live wire, fully charged
with high-voltage electricity. He managed a grunt of
surprise as the hammering force swept through him, a
grunt that became a yelp of pain and then silence as his
voice fled him.

He tried to pull himself free, but couldn't. His
body was in revolt, the muscles refusing to obey his
commands. He could not speak or move, and even the
beating of his heart seemed to have stilled. The world
seemed poised to go away.

"Xander!" Cordy screamed.

And then he was somewhere else. Somewhere
else, and *someone* else.

Or many someones.

"Remarkable. Your champions are making progress,"
Cagliostro said from his chair. His voice still echoed
slightly, but the gunslinger had fallen silent. Evidently,
the battle that Giles could hear raging outside was
commanding more and more of the alchemist's attention. "You've trained her well," he told the Watcher.
"You've given her a kind of greatness."

Giles allowed himself to shake his head. "No," he
said, with complete honesty. "Any greatness Buffy has
is of her own making."

Cagliostro didn't believe him and said so. "I'd

entertained fantasies of taking her alive," he said. "I've long wanted to study the inner workings of the Slayer. The blood, the nerves, the elemental tissues—they really must be most remarkable."

"You'll never take her alive," Giles said.

"Defiance?"

"Not defiance," Giles said. "Simple fact."

Scarcely had he spoken the words when the booth door flew off its hinges. It bounced and spun as it flew, freed by one savage kick from a nicely booted foot. Startled, both men turned to face the opening, and in it, the trim outline of a girl. Behind her was darkness, filled with half-seen images of battle and thick with the sounds of combat.

"All right, mister," Buffy said. "Fun's fun, but the show's over. I need my librarian back."

Giles had never been so happy to see her in all his life, and his joy was dimmed only slightly when the nameless gunslinger pressed a loaded pistol against the back of his head.

Willow dropped to her knees. No one seemed to notice—not Buffy, not Angel, not any of the spectral horde who defended the projection booth. She half-crawled, half-walked, and let the tide of battle sweep over her, unmindful and uncaring. They were focused entirely on Buffy and Angel. Whoever or whatever commanded them must have decided that she didn't matter. Whether deliberately or by utter lack of concern, she was being allowed to retreat.

She hated that. She hated being useless, being the

weak link. Most of all, she hated retreating, but there was nothing she could do.

Then she realized that there *was*.

Cagliostro stood. Still connected to the projector via the glowing umbilical cord, he bowed politely, a complete bow, and smiled at Buffy. "Well played," he said. "The trap is sprung."

"Trap?" Buffy said. "You've got to be kidding. This wasn't a trap." She raised the two blades.

"Oh?" he asked.

"I've read up on you," she said. "I've asked around. You're just a blowhard trying to make the best of a bad situation. I figure, you didn't think I'd come running, at least not quite as fast." She paused. "Giles, you okay?"

"I'm fine, Buffy," came the Watcher's response.

"That could change," Cagliostro said ominously.

Every muscle in Buffy's body was vibrating with tension. "I wouldn't advise it," she said. "Now, tell the cowboy to put down his gun, and we can end this easy."

"I think not," Cagliostro said. Without the slightest show of concern, he continued. "You'll put down your weapons. Surrender to me, and I'll grant your Watcher his life, though not his freedom. If not . . ." He shrugged.

Buffy scarcely looked as she threw the *boka*. The casual toss was dead on target, though, and felled the phantom gunslinger. "There," the Slayer said. "We'll do it the hard way, then."

"The *very* hard way," Cagliostro said, as even more

agents materialized: the six bikers who had given her and Angel such a hard time the night before. They arranged themselves between her and the alchemist.

"He dies, you die," Buffy promised. The odds were terrible, but she knew she could beat them. Only one question made her pause.

Would she be freeing Giles, or ensuring his death?

It was as if Xander were everywhere at once, or nowhere at all. He seemed to be seeing the world from a thousand different angles, all at the same time, and his hearing was even worse. The overwhelming rush of information seemed like enough to make his head explode, only he didn't seem to have a head anymore. He didn't seem to have anything but his thoughts and his senses, all of which worked with what had to be superhuman clarity.

He saw Mr. Snyder, alone in the Snydermobile, watching *Double Drunken Dragon Kung Fu Fight* and chuckling as he nibbled a corn dog.

He saw Joyce Summers shake the shoulder of her sleeping escort, and he heard her worried voice ask, "Barney? Are you all right, Barney?"

He saw the girl with purple hair lead her fatso boyfriend toward the drive-in exit, and heard her angrily telling him about her encounter with some uppity blond chick with an axe. If he could have, Xander would have nodded. The Magic Box girl had to be talking about Buffy.

He saw Willow, moving fast in a half crouch, crawl between parked cars and approach the projection booth from its blind side, where the long cables that powered the place hung low.

And then he heard a familiar voice say the kind of words he'd heard so many times before: "He dies, you die."

"Buffy?" he heard himself ask.

The bikers had been approaching, but now they froze in place. So did the replacement gunslinger who had suddenly materialized behind Giles. Even Cagliostro seemed locked in place, but his paralysis was less complete. Where the others were frozen like a video still frame, Cagliostro had merely paused. An expression of absolute confusion formed on his aristocratic features, and he licked his lips as he looked from side to side.

"Buffy?" he said. "Giles? What's going on here?"

Buffy blinked, completely dumbfounded. The centuries-old master mage, philosopher, and politician had spoken in a different voice, the voice of a confused teenager.

"Xander?" she asked.

"Buffy, what's—"

Giles interrupted. "The projector, Buffy. It's the projector. That's the secret of his power."

"Of course," Buffy said.

"No," Cagliostro said, speaking in his own voice again. "No, you—"

Willow had watched Buffy enter the projection booth. Angel stood with his back to the door, serving as rear guard, fighting off an army of apparitions that sought to follow the Slayer inside. Willow watched as Angel's arms rose and fell in merciless, killing strokes. Heads and arms and other body parts flew, then faded into nothingness. It was like seeing Horatio at the bridge, or the last stand at the Alamo. With his back covered, the vampire could make his stand and hold it for a very long time.

At least long enough for Willow to be of some help.

She still held the petite axe, and she kept it at the ready to defend herself, but there was no need. No one and nothing tried to stop her as she made her way to the rear wall of the projection building. Heavy cables entered the structure through fixtures on the blind wall. Willow eyed them. Her own words came back to her: "It looks like some kind of fiber-optic network," she'd told Buffy as they'd noticed the silver cords that led to the projector's rays.

Whatever the system Cagliostro used, the projection equipment was part of it. Projection equipment needed power. Actually slicing the cables with her axe would be dangerous, even fatal, but if she could *throw* the weapon . . .

Willow raised the axe and took aim.

Buffy's machete really wasn't well balanced for throwing, but she made do. Only one of the paired projectors was running, which made her choice of target easy. She cast the machete like a dagger, fast and hard. Heavy tempered steel, honed to a razor edge, buried itself with gratifying effect into the projector's switch box.

Lightning struck. Long, liquid sparks sprayed and splashed as the machine's housing sundered. They were nothing like the pale tendrils that Buffy had seen outdoors, but savage, searing bolts that split the air and burned it with their passage. The projection shack filled with the stink of ozone as the projector shuddered to a halt and died.

Cagliostro died too.

He died screaming, with the accumulated fury and frustration of a life that had gone on for entirely too long. Haloed in electrical fire, he shook and convulsed, and then seemed to collapse into himself in obedience of some strange geometry. As Buffy watched, he dwindled and twisted in ways that made her eyes hurt. It was as if he were falling away from her in all directions at once, only to be lost in an infinite distance.

She tore her gaze from where he'd been and turned to Giles. They were alone in the small room now; the bikers and gunfighter had vanished as thoroughly as their creator, albeit with less spectacle. Dark spots danced in her vision as she reached to untie his bonds, and it took her a moment to realize that they were gone too.

"They belonged to the cowboy," Giles told her as he stood.

"Gunslinger," Buffy corrected him, but she hugged the Watcher, hard enough to make him gasp. "You're safe? He didn't hurt you?"

"I'm fine," Giles said, wriggling free. "But what on earth is that cacophony?"

It sounded like a hundred car horns were blaring,

and when Buffy and Giles stepped outside, the reason was obvious. The screen had gone black. Angel, certain now that the war was over, offered an explanation. "I think they want their money back," he said.

"But—but—everyone got in free!" Buffy said slowly.

Epilogue

"... That's when the screen went dark," Willow said. She seemed disappointed. "Before I could even throw the axe, I mean."

"Don't worry, Will," Buffy said. "It was the right idea. You just weren't the only one to have it."

"Well, sure, but—"

"Next time, you can save the day," Buffy said. "Really, I promise."

Willow beamed.

They were back in the school library, seated again at the table. Giles was watching nervously as Xander examined the lens that Giles had retrieved from the ruined projector. Perhaps three inches across, it was thick and convex on both sides. It was heavy, too— much heavier than ordinary optical glass. Whatever it had been crafted of, the substance didn't seem to bend light—an odd property for a projector lens.

"So that's the little toy that caused so much trouble," Xander said. He plucked the bit of crystal from the velvet-lined box where Giles was keeping it. "Doesn't look like much," he said.

"It's only a tool," Giles said, still watching Xander carefully. "Think, Xander. How much use would a lens be at a puppet show, or in the days before magick lanterns? Balsamo's basic abilities were his own, I think, though we may never know how he gained them. The lens was but a means to focus and direct them."

"I thought he said the Hellmouth—"

"I said, *basic* abilities," Giles reminded him. "The lens gave him focus, but the Hellmouth made him stronger." He paused. "Even so, be careful with that. I want very much to study it, which means I don't want you to damage it."

"Yeah, yeah, yeah," Xander said. "Anyone ever tell you that you worry too much, G-man?"

"Maybe it's diamond?" Cordelia asked. It was like her to ignore the most interesting aspect and focus instead on the most materialistic one.

Giles shook his head. "A form of crystal, I think. Possibly Latverian."

"Where do you think he got it?" Willow asked.

"I suspect he made it," Giles said. He claimed the stone and eyed its rim. Minute symbols were etched there in an undecipherable language. "Latverian crystals are sensitive to astral energies, and he probably began with one of those."

It was Monday. Sunday had been a day of recovery and happiness. The news had spread that all thirty of the sleepers had awakened, and that no more had been found. News media were speculating that it was some form of food poisoning and had turned their attention to the mysterious doings at the drive-in. Oddly, no one seemed to draw a connection between the two events; the team consensus was that Cagliostro's charming disclaimer had endured past his death.

"How is your mother, Buffy?" Giles asked.

"Mom? Fine. Just embarrassed about falling asleep at the movies," Buffy said. "I'm surprised she was there at all, after all this Barney character's talk about 'something bad' happening years ago." She looked disgusted. "Turns out that 'something bad' in grown-up talk means 'losing your investment capital.' But everyone is fine. Mom, Jonathan, Aura, everyone. There's some bellhop who says he's going to write a book about the whole thing."

"What about you, Xander?" Giles asked. "That must have been quite an experience."

"Oh, yeah," Xander said. He mock-shuddered. "Kind of creepy, really. Going to be a while before I sleep well. Not that I'm complaining."

"I'd like to discuss it with you at length. You actually stepped outside your body without the years of training that such things require," Giles said.

Willow offered up a theory of what had happened, elaborating on what she'd discussed before: Cagliostro's web of sorcery was something very much like an astral Internet. As long as his was the only waking mind online, he ruled the network.

"But when Xander put himself online, it was like

adding a second file server without the right trafficking protocols," she said. "The network locked up and the system crashed, at least for a moment."

"Of course," Giles said.

"You didn't understand a word of that, did you?" Buffy asked him.

Giles didn't answer directly. "All that matters is that it gave you the opening you needed," he said. "And whatever it was that Xander did, it was astoundingly dangerous." He placed the lens in its box. "I'm certainly glad that Cordelia thought to use a pillow for insulation when she pulled you free."

"Well, it's like she keeps telling us—," Xander began to say.

"I'm not stupid," Cordelia interrupted.

ABOUT THE AUTHOR

Pierce Askegren was born in Pennsylvania and lives today in Virginia, with many intermediate whistle-stops along the way (his daddy was a railroad man). At various points in his so-called career, Pierce has been a convenience store clerk, bookstore manager, technical editor, logistics analyst, and writer for business proposals and industrial instruction materials. At one point he knew an alarming amount about wireless communications protocols.

Pierce has written extensively for Marvel Comics characters, having authored or coauthored five novels featuring Spider-Man, the Fantastic Four, the Hulk and the rest of the gang. He has also worked on other series, including *Gateway to the Stars*, a novel based on the popular Traveller role-playing game, and *Alias*. He is also the author of *Inconstant Moon*, a trilogy of original science-fiction novels, the most recent of which is *Exit Strategy*.

"I'm the Slayer. Slay-er. Chosen One? She who hangs out a lot in cemeteries? Ask around. Look it up: 'Slayer *comma* The.'"

—Buffy, "Doomed"

INTO EVERY GENERATION,

A SLAYER IS BORN

Seven years, 144 episodes, three Slayers, two networks, two vampires with souls(!), two Watchers, three principals, two pigs, one Master, one Mayor, countless potentials: It all adds up to one hit show.

The Watcher's Guides, Volumes 1–3, are the *complete* collection of authorized companions to the hit show *Buffy the Vampire Slayer*. Don't be caught dead without them!

Buffy the Vampire Slayer™

Into every generation,
a Slayer is born . . .

Before there was Buffy, there were other Slayers—called to protect the world from the undead. Led by their Watchers, they have served as our defense—across the globe and throughout history.

In these collections of short stories written by best-selling authors, travel through time to these other Slayers. From France in the fourteenth century to Iowa in the 1980s, the young women have protected the world. Their stories—and legacies—are unforgettable.

You've waited long enough. Find out what happened to Buffy *after* the Hellmouth ate Sunnydale, in this exciting new book!

Picking up just after the series finale, Queen of the Slayers *is an exclusive look into the much-missed characters' lives.*

With the closing of the Hellmouth and the "awakening" of hundreds of potential Slayers, Buffy Summers thought she had overturned the Slayer's self-sacrifice and earned herself a much-deserved break of normalcy. But the thrill of victory is short-lived. The Forces of Darkness are not ones to graciously accept defeat.

Willow's magickal distribution of the Slayer essence left girls across the world discovering their latent power. But soon Buffy hears word that a number of the fresh Slayers are being coerced to join an army of Slayers—governed by the mysterious "Queen of the Slayers," an awesome evil determined to claim the intoxicating Slayer essence for herself. The deciding apocalypse is drawing near. Alliances are formed and loyalties betrayed as it comes down to Slayer versus Slayer, leading to an ultimate battle of champions—from Buffy's past and present.